TICKET TO RIDE

TICKET TO RIDE

ED GORMAN

THORNDIKE
CHIVERS

This Large Print edition is published by Thorndike Press, Waterville, Maine, USA and by BBC Audiobooks Ltd, Bath, England.
Thorndike Press, a part of Gale, Cengage Learning.
A Sam McCain Mystery.

The text of this Large Print edition is unabridged.
Other aspects of the book may vary from the original edition.
Set in 16 pt. Plantin.
Printed on permanent paper.

LIBRARY OF CONGRESS CATALOGING-IN-PUBLICATION DATA

Gorman, Edward.
  Ticket to ride / by Ed Gorman. — Large print ed.
    p. cm. — (Thorndike Press large print mystery)
  "A Sam McCain Mystery."
  ISBN-13: 978-1-4104-2425-9 (alk. paper)
  ISBN-10: 1-4104-2425-1 (alk. paper)
  1. McCain, Sam (Fictitious character)—Fiction. 2. Private investigators—Iowa—Fiction. 3. Iowa—Fiction. 4. Large type books. I. Title.
PS3557.O759T53 2010
813'.54—dc22
                                      2009046716

BRITISH LIBRARY CATALOGUING-IN-PUBLICATION DATA AVAILABLE

Published in 2010 in the U.S. by arrangement with Pegasus Books LLC.
Published in 2010 in the U.K. by arrangement with the author.

U.K. Hardcover: 978 1 408 47838 7 (Chivers Large Print)
U.K. Softcover: 978 1 40847839 4 (Camden Large Print)

Printed in the United States of America
1 2 3 4 5 6 7 14 13 12 11 10

To some of the good ones along the way:

Linda Ashley
Terry Butler
Bonnie Cain
Connie DeVore
Sister Mary Emmanuel
Bunny Heskje
Doug Humble
Ted McCord
John McHugh
Ed Popelka
Steve Schwartz
Clete Sharp
Linda Shaw
Jim Siepman
Tom Spaight
Judy Stevenson
Jim Stuckenschneider
Mary Carol Travis
Dick Weltz

I'd like to thank Beth Morgan, who oversees the most informative Website of all for those of us who suffer the incurable cancer multiple myeloma.

As always, my thanks to Linda Siebels, whose first read and first edit of my books is invaluable.

*So let us not talk falsely now
the hour is getting late*
— Bob Dylan
"All Along the Watchtower"

It was quite a summer for news. President Lyndon Johnson's effigy was burned on eight different campuses because of the escalating Vietnam war; the number of men drafted per month doubled to 35,000; Medicare was established; *Mariner 4* sent back our first pictures of Mars; people who liked folk music were still mad at Bob Dylan for going electric; and for the first and only time, Walter Cronkite on the CBS Evening News mentioned our little town of Black River Falls, Iowa.

The story dealt with a rather befuddled police chief named Clifford Sykes, Jr., who had joined forces with an equally befuddled local minister, H. Dobson Cartwright, to rid our town of sin by putting all the high school–age boys with long hair in jail. They would be released only when they signed a "contract" guaranteeing that they would get their hair cut within twenty-four hours. Cartwright was of the opinion that the Beatles were instruments of Satan and that long hair on boys was a sign that they had handed their souls over to the Prince of Darkness himself.

It was hard to tell who resented the arrest decree more, the boys or their parents. The CBS story focused on the near-riot that occurred in front of the new police station on the night of July 23 when at least three hundred parents and their long-haired offspring demanded the badge of the aforementioned Clifford Sykes, Jr.

Also present were representatives of the state attorney general, the ACLU, and three members of LEGALIZE POT NOW! The assistant attorney general and the woman from the ACLU addressed the crowd and said that their boys had nothing to fear, that what the police chief and the minister advocated was clearly unconstitutional, and that whoever was hurling rocks at the police station should cease and desist. The three scruffy teenagers with the marijuana organization just watched the proceedings with very glassy eyes.

Now if you were working for the Chamber of Commerce and were trying to attract business to Black River Falls, this was not exactly the kind of story you wanted publicized. The sheriff was clearly a rube and the reverend a crackpot. Walter Cronkite, usually the most proper of men, couldn't resist a wry smile just before he said goodnight.

That was the amusing part of the summer.

The less amusing part had to do with the doubled draft numbers. Our little town had already lost four men in Vietnam over the past two years. While the majority of folks never questioned what the government did — I suspect it's that way in most countries — there were some of us who had a whole hell of a lot of questions about why we were there.

And we decided it was time to ask those questions in a public way.

PART ONE

1

By the time the fight started, I was all speeched out. Even though I was against the war in Vietnam, an hour and a half of listening to the same arguments had turned principle into monotony. The irony was that I was one of the rally organizers.

"How come you keep sighing?" Molly Weaver whispered. "Pay attention."

In a previous life, the newest addition to the *Black River Falls Clarion* had likely been a nun of nasty disposition. We'd been struggling through a relationship for the past two months, both of us trying to recover from being dumped by people without the wisdom to love us and love us utterly. With her dark hair, slender form, bright blue eyes, and quick deft smile, Molly gave the impression of what my father would call "a gal who just likes to have fun." But Molly's fetching looks were misleading. She was like dating a character from an Ibsen play.

Tonight's date had taken us to a small rally on the back steps of the Presbyterian church. There were maybe thirty people sweating it out in the eighty-five-degree dusk. Three speakers had preceded the present one. They were as sweaty as rock singers after an hour on stage. But they were only opening acts for the star.

I suppose I had to consider the possibility that I disliked Harrison Doran because I was jealous of him. For one thing, he was not stuck on the lower floors of life's elevator. He was six-two to my five-six. He had also, though not necessarily in this order, appeared on stage with his good friend Joan Baez at her anti-war concert; spoken at the demonstration in Washington, D.C., in front of 25,000 people; and shared a radio interview with his close friend Norman Mailer. Doran was also due, at age twenty-five, to inherit somewhere in the vicinity of ten million dollars from his father. He had become a star in our little community. Girls trailed him everywhere.

So why would I be jealous? Me? Sam McCain?

The people in the front row held lighted candles in the vermilion moments before full darkness; the people in the second row held bobbing signs.

With his long blond locks and beard and his quarterback size, Doran did have a certain theatrical style, the kind of cavalier who also had a doctorate from Yale. Oh, yes, the town ladies loved him, though after a month of being dazzled some of them were starting to find his narcissism overwhelming. Not Molly. Molly had once dragged me to a dinner in his honor and we'd had the misfortune of sitting near him. I should say *I* had the misfortune. Molly was transfixed. That she had a crush on him was easy to see.

The speech droned on. I was thinking about the double feature at the drive-in, two Hammer films both with Peter Cushing. They'd be starting in half an hour. I was hoping we'd be there in time. I hated being late to a movie and as much as I was against the war, *She* and *The Evil of Frankenstein* sounded a lot better than sweating it out here.

He was just there suddenly, Lou Bennett, or as he prefers to be called, *Colonel* Lou Bennett. It was a sneak attack. The crowd had been listening to Doran, not paying attention to the fact that a form even darker than the shadows was moving to the top of the concrete steps where a stand-up microphone had been placed.

Bennett wasn't threatening at first. He just walked over to Doran and stood next to him, a rangy, gray-haired muscular man in a blue golf shirt and chinos. You could feel how the crowd seized up when they saw him. After glancing at the retired Army man, Doran tried to keep talking but quickly gave it up. "Is there something I can do for you, Colonel?"

"Yes, there is, Mr. Doran. I'd like you to give me the opportunity to rebut what you're saying. I think the people need to hear the other side."

Stray boos came now. There was going to be a confrontation. When my stomach knots a certain way, it's never wrong.

"We hear your side of the story everywhere we go," Doran snapped. "You've got the whole government and the whole news media behind you."

"That's because they know the truth." Only now was Bennett's voice getting tight.

"This is a bogus war, Colonel. I don't want innocent children murdered in my name." Everybody started clapping and yelling approval. Hell, even I did. "Now I'd appreciate it if you'd leave and let me finish my speech."

That was when Bennett shoved Doran

aside and grabbed the microphone. "My son Bryce gave his life in Vietnam last year and you people are trampling on his grave."

And there it was. The unspoken had now been spoken. The death of his son in a far alien place called Da Nang. All over the country this rage and hatred was causing rifts between friends and even family members. Bennett felt the rage and hatred because of his son; we felt it because of the slaughter on both sides and the folly of the whole goddamned thing. Another war. A good share of the country seemed to need one from time to time. There was no other way to explain how easily they could be led into it. And we knew damned well, it would keep expanding.

"Go home, Bennett! You don't belong here!" somebody in the crowd shouted.

"You're a pig, Bennett!" somebody else bellered.

"Your son died because of people like you! You killed your son!" Ugly as it was, the third cry silenced everybody for a moment.

Bennett's entire body jerked as if he'd been physically wounded. He gaped right, then left, as if he expected somebody to come and rescue him. He looked older, too, and despite the gym-hardened sixty-year-old body, suddenly he seemed frail.

This wasn't what I'd come to hear. I'd never liked Bennett, but I didn't want to see him ripped apart.

Doran made a lunge for him, but Bennett had enough strength to shove him back.

"You people should go home and get down on your knees and thank the good Lord for the lives our fighting men have given you." At this point he didn't need a microphone. His voice was carrying far past the parking lot behind us. And then he broke: "That's what my son gave his life for. For you and you and you. And what the hell do you give him?" He was sobbing now, his voice cracking. "And what the hell do *you* give him? You give him this!"

I was pretty sure everybody else was responding the way I was. He'd shocked us. And not because he was the bully who'd commandeered the microphone but because he was this asshole who for at least one startling moment was not an asshole at all. He was just this poor guy who'd lost his son. It didn't matter how he felt about the war in general. The war had taken his son. The son who'd spent his life growing up in Black River Falls. The son who'd been a nice young kid. He'd married a town girl and then went to war and died.

The only light was from the candles and

the lights inside the church that filled the glass rear entrance doors. Bennett staggered around like Lear, knocking over the microphone as he did so. Screeching assaulted the steamy air as the microphone bounced off the concrete entranceway.

Nobody was moving to help Bennett. He needed to be assisted off the platform. He just kept stumbling around. I wondered if he'd had some kind of breakdown.

I said nothing to Molly. I just worked my way through the people in front of me and rushed to the steps. I was almost there when I saw Doran finally move. He walked over to Bennett and tried to put his hand on the man's shoulder. And that was when it started. Bennett swiveled around like a spooked animal. But that wasn't all he did. He brought up a massive fist and slammed it hard and unerringly into Doran's face. Doran screamed. Actually screamed. I wondered if his nose was broken.

Doran started to pull away but Bennett followed him and hit him twice more, once again in the face and then in the stomach. I was able to shove Bennett so that Doran would be out of target range.

Bennett was shouting at me. He was also swinging at me but I stayed below the punches and just kept slamming the palms of my hands into his chest to force him back. By now three men among the protestors had jumped up next to us and helped me restrain him.

I glanced behind me once. Molly was nursing the prone figure of Harrison Doran. In that millisecond, I realized that she'd finally managed to hook up with him. I'd sensed that was where it was heading — she'd told me she'd once plastered her bedroom walls with photographs of Fabian; Doran had taken old Fabe's place.

A siren. The police station was only three blocks away. Somebody had warned the police that this sanctioned protest was turning bad.

The men had managed to push Bennett up against the entrance doors where they held his arms so he couldn't swing. He wasn't screaming now, he was sobbing again. I wished he'd been screaming. It was a hell of a lot easier to take.

The candles were all out. The small gathering stood in broken little groups talking quietly. Seeing Bennett snap as he had wasn't good for political morale. Bennett was a bastard, but I pitied him; and Molly's nursing Doran struck me as a betrayal. There was a quarter moon and the lawn had been mowed today and I wanted to float away on the summer sweetness of the scent.

Then I heard him: "You take your hands off the man or I'll throw all of you in jail."

Clifford Sykes, Jr., known to most townspeople as Cliffie, had arrived in his tan uniform with the big Western star on his breast pocket and his campaign hat slanted on his thick head. In case you missed the Western motif, he wore his Sam Browne low on his hip like the gunfighters in cowboy movies. He didn't have framed photos of Fabian on his office walls, but I bet he had a few of Glenn Ford.

For a while there, Cliffie had started acting like a serious police officer. He'd rescued two people from a burning car, told a deputy to knock off the racial slurs, and had let his cousin Jane Sykes — the district attorney I'd fallen in love with; the district attorney who'd broken my heart — actually give him and his staff a few lessons in police conduct. But when Jane decided to return to Chicago and her ex-husband, Cliffie seemed to forget everything he'd learned.

He elbowed through the gathering and then hurried up the steps. "I should've figured you'd be involved in this, McCain. The only thing I'll say for the judge is she sure as hell wouldn't hook up with a bunch of Communists like this."

He was moving all the time he was yelling at me. The men had unhanded Bennett, but Bennett hadn't moved. He'd quit sobbing, but he stared straight down and made tiny whimpering sounds.

"Lou, Lou, what the hell did these bastards do to you?"

No response. I moved closer and that was when I saw, peripherally, Doran limping away. Molly had her shoulder under his arm and her hand on his stomach. The shoulder I understood. The stomach looked like the female equivalent of a cheap feel.

"Lou, Lou, you got to look at me, Lou!" As he said this, Cliffie snapped on a silver flashlight the size of a ball bat and waved the beam so his officer would come up here and help him.

"Maybe he needs a doctor."

Cliffie's facial expression was lost in the shadows but his voice was clear: "McCain, I'm ordering you to disperse this crowd and you to go with them. That permit I gave you is cancelled. And you can tell that to the beatnik pastor too."

Then he leaned closer, his beer breath scouring my face and said: "That pastor. He's no pastor."

Pastor Gerard had replaced Pastor Beaton. Gerard was only twenty-eight, and he and his wife were known to serve wine at their parties and listen to jazz. Beaton had been seventy-nine when he finally retired. A town wag had once claimed that Beaton had fallen into a coma around age fifty-five, only nobody had ever noticed. Cliffie had been heard to call Gerard and his wife "bohemians," which confused some of the locals of Czech heritage. "Now you get them the hell out of here, you hear me?"

I faced the few remaining protestors. I didn't have to say anything. They'd heard Cliffie bellering. I saw Molly helping Doran into her car.

The odd thing was that after that first jab of jealousy, I found myself not caring. Molly and I had been going nowhere, anyway.

I was fifteen feet from my red Ford ragtop when a small red Triumph shot into sight so fast I wondered if it would be able to stop before it overshot the parking lot.

The woman who climbed from it shouted, "Where is he, McCain?"

"Cliffie has him. Your father's not doing very well."

"You had to have this goddamned thing, didn't you?"

Usually I would have argued with the arrogant Linda Raines, but her father was sick for one thing, and for another I had no energy for it.

Her face was lighted suddenly by head-lights. I turned to see a red MG pulling up just a few feet from us. David Raines, Linda's husband, did his best James Bond by leaping over the car door and hurrying to us. "Linda! Wait!" But she was already running toward her father.

"This was a stupid goddamn idea, Mc-Cain. You can tell all the people on your stupid little committee that I said that." He set off after his wife.

I watched her rush across the lawn toward the rear entrance of the church. She was a small, finely made woman of thirty. She'd been a year ahead of me in high school. Her dark good looks made her popular despite her famous dark moods. I'd been told that her moods had calmed over the years, but not her intensity.

She was gone into the shadows, leaving me to stand there and think about Lou Bennett and being forced to see him as a human being instead of a demon, which I resented. He'd spent his years promoting his friends to the city council and getting his way more often than not. I never forgave him for humiliating my father one night at a council meeting. I was twelve or thirteen. We lived in the poorest part of the city, the part called the Hills. My father wanted to know when a long-promised skating rink would be built for people on our side of town. He said, "It ain't right to keep promising and not making good on it." I was embarrassed; I still remember the shame I felt. And then I hated myself for feeling shame. My father had only gone through eighth grade in the Depression. He read a lot, but every so often an "ain't" would slip out. Lou Bennett stood up in the front row and said, "Well, we sure ain't going to break our word no more, Mr. McCain." I imagined that my father could still hear the laughter of that night; I still could. It was one of those moments nobody but my father and I would remember. It was a moment I'd never forget.

2

"You don't put salt in your beer anymore, huh?"

"No, I read this article about salt intake."

Kenny Thibodeau, our town's soft-core pornographer and writer of tall tales for men's magazines, looked across the table and smiled. "I don't have to tell you about 'articles,' do I?"

"This one's legit, Kenny. By a doctor."

"I'm a doctor."

"Yeah, of 'sexology.'"

When not writing books with titles such as *Satan's Sisters* and *Pagan Lesbians,* or "true" articles such as "Hitler's Love Maidens" and "The Wild Rampage of the Sex-Crazed Pirate Women!" Kenny writes a sex advice column under the name Dr. William Ambrose, "PhD and renowned Sexologist." He cribs all his material from the *Playboy* Sex Advice column. His real name appears on none of this material. He's saving that for the serious novels I know he has in him, though I'm not sure he himself knows that anymore. There's one more reason for the pen names. J. Edgar Hoover and politically ambitious DAs across the country have been trying to send soft-core editors and writers to prison. Two publishers were already serving time. Their number-one target is comedian Lenny Bruce, of course. He was recently sentenced to jail again.

"So what happened at the demonstration tonight? I'd have been there except Sue had a doctor's appointment in Iowa City and her car's in the garage. I had to give her a ride."

In high school Kenny's idols were Jack Kerouac and Allen Ginsberg. He was messianic about the entire Beat movement. I was his only convert. I even subscribed to the *Evergreen Review,* which was the bible of the movement. One summer Kenny drove to the Beat Mecca, San Francisco, where he spent three days running in City Lights Bookstore. This was where he also met the soft-core publisher who convinced him he could make a reasonable living writing the stuff. Until two years ago Kenny still wore the uniform: the goatee, the dark clothes, the hipster talk. Then he met Sue and she changed him, which explained the

31

short hair, blue button-down shirt, and chinos he was wearing tonight.

"Bennett really flipped out, huh?"

I described what happened. Including the angry appearance of Linda Raines.

"Yeah. She gives bitches a bad name." He stood up. "Have to hit the can."

I gave myself over to the pleasures of Nealy's, the front part of which used to be a drugstore and the back half of which is a tavern. The east wall in the front still has the old glassed-in wooden cabinetry used for the pharmacy. There's a soda fountain across from it where four or five generations of blue-collar boys and girls made each other happy and broke each other's hearts.

You'll find the town's two finest pinball machines here, as well as a pretty good shuffleboard table. There are booths along one wall where you can bring the plump roast beef sandwiches — their only menu item — and relax. It's a workingman's place, so country music fights rock for dominance on the jukebox and three blackboards chart the betting on various baseball, football, and basketball games. When Cassius Clay came on the scene, they started betting on boxing, too.

After Jane Sykes decided to go back to the husband she'd divorced, I sort of took up residence here. One night I even got belligerent and got into a fistfight out on the sidewalk in back. Since I'd started it, I was on an informal probation here for two weeks. It was like being back in Catholic school after you got caught dropping a water balloon out of the second-story window. I apologized to the guy and we were now friendly if not friends, though I still wince when I see him. Not the finest entry on the biographical sheet.

Kenny returned bearing two glasses of beer. He stretched out in the booth. "What a family. Bennett and all his military bullshit and Linda acting like Scarlett O'Hara and the kid — Bryce — I had some hope for him, though. I'd see him at the library a lot when he was in high school."

"I thought he was a football player."

"Just because you don't like sports, you think everybody who plays is an idiot." Kenny loved football games.

"You're right. That was a stupid thing to say."

"God, I must've caught you on an off night."

"Nah. I'm just worried about my dad. I was just being sanctimonious because I'm in a bad mood, I guess."

"I need to pick up Sue pretty soon here.

Maybe you should stop by and see your folks."

Gloom tends to paralyze me. I can sit and brood for long angry hours. Between the ruined peace rally and my mom's whispers over the phone this afternoon, I felt alone and useless. Kenny's suggestion got me going again.

"Thanks for saying that."

"Saying what?"

"To go see my folks."

"Yeah, that was a pretty brilliant idea if I say so myself."

"Make a joke, asshole. It's what I needed to hear."

He pushed out of the booth and stood up. "I'm going to start charging you for these ideas I have." Then he was gone.

There was a time when my mother was eager to tell my father which TV show she wanted to watch. And he was just as eager to tell her which show *he* preferred. As near as I could figure, they pretty much split even on their respective TV choices.

But now as they sat in the living room, I saw they were watching a Western show called *Laredo,* which meant that my mother would not be seeing *Bewitched,* which was on at the same time. She wanted the shrunken man next to her on the couch to see whatever he wanted. Though neither of us ever said it out loud, my mother and I knew that my father's heart condition would take his life any time now. Of course the doctors had told him three different times over the past four years that he was about to die. But this time it felt different. It felt scary.

I'd come in the back door and stood in the darkness of the dining room just watching them sit there together. She had his hand in her lap. She'd told me a few days ago that she spent most of her time thinking back over their lives. How they'd grown up in the Hills and how they'd gone dancing every weekend and won prizes they were so good, and how my father doted on the three of us kids and stood crying outside our bedrooms the night he got his draft notice five weeks after Pearl Harbor. She said he wasn't worried about dying; he was worried that something would happen to us while he was gone. And then after the war getting a job so good at the plant that they were able to buy a modest house in a respectable neighborhood and live out at least a few of those American dreams the politicians were always bragging about. The most devout dream of all in Black River

Falls was to escape the poverty of the Hills.

He'd lost nearly twenty-five pounds and he'd never been a big man anyway, a scrappy Irisher whose two favorite pastimes were bowling and reading Westerns. Watching him now, how even the slightest move either caused him to gasp or wince, I was afraid I was going to cry. I was a child again facing the unthinkable. I'd come here after seeing Lou Bennett fall apart. I suppose I wanted to reassure myself that my own dad was all right.

When I walked into the room, my mom smiled. In the flashing colors from the TV screen I was able to see my father's face clearly now. He was asleep. My mom put a finger to her lips. I sat down next to my dad and slid my arm around him. Part of the time I watched the screen, though none of the frantic storyline registered. But mostly I looked at my dad, the TV beam tinting his bald pate, the white werewolf hair sprouting from his ear and the scents of him I'd known since my earliest days. I remembered him when he came home from the war. I'd never felt more loved or doted on, nor had my sister or brother. We were a family again. The years the war had put on my mother vanished. She was a young woman again.

I started fighting tears then, couldn't help

it. The old Verlaine line always came back to me like a bitter plea: *Why are we born to suffer and die?* There was no explanation for life, let alone for death.

I reached across the back of my father and took my mother's hand. She nodded. She'd given up her own reluctance to cry. Her eyes gleamed.

I left to the sounds of a gunfight and then horses riding fast out of town.

3

"I get real nervous."

"Uh-huh."

"You know, maybe this time they won't get together at all."

"Umm-hmm."

"Turk says my breasts aren't as big as hers."

That got my attention. Mention of Turk always gets my attention.

"He told you that?"

"Uh-huh."

"Did you slap him?"

"No. It kind of hurt my feelings, but then Turk always says he's just being honest when he says stuff like that."

Well, I thought, then maybe it's time I laid a little truth on Turk.

Jamie Newton became my secretary in a version of a slave auction. I'd represented her father in a boundary dispute. It was a long shot and we lost. He couldn't afford to pay me, so he gave me his teenaged daughter as a part-time secretary. She was quite a looker. She could have modeled for half of those paperback covers depicting ripe young teenage girls who used their jailbait wiles to seduce men into killing people for them. But that was only how she looked. She was actually sweet and considerate. The problem was that she was also sort of dumb. She couldn't type, file, or take telephone messages with any precision. Twice a day I want to fire her, but I know that she would never understand. All her life, people have told her how stupid she is. Firing her would only confirm her worst fears. She now worked full-time for me.

"Maybe you should be honest with *him* sometime."

My office is about the size of two prison cells. It's furnished with two desks and two chairs I bought over the years at county condemnation sales. There are two filing cabinets that I bought at Sears and a bookcase that I'd had growing up. Since our desks faced each other, Jamie didn't have any trouble watching me.

"I wouldn't want to hurt his feelings. Plus I really can't think of anything wrong with him." Those gentle blue eyes stayed on mine. "You look mad or something, Mr. C."

"I'm just thinking he shouldn't talk to you that way."

"But he's going to be famous someday. With his band. I'll be sitting home in front of the TV and there he'll be on Dick Clark. The Surfer Bums. It's such a great name. That's why we go to all those beach movies at the drive-in. So he can learn how to dress like a surfer and stuff." Then: "But he always laughs at me because I get so scared. You know, when Frankie and Annette have all their fights I worry that they'll never get back together."

Oh, Jamie, goddammit. You could do so much better than that asshole.

"And I like Annette so much that when he says her breasts are bigger than mine it doesn't really bother me that much, Mr. C."

The "Mr. C," by the way, comes from the Perry Como TV show. She thought it was pretty cool how all the people on the show addressed Como that way. No, my name doesn't start with a "C," but that's a minor detail to Jamie.

"Are you still giving him money?"

She blushed. "Well, he needs to buy surfer clothes. He has to go to Cedar Rapids to buy them. Things're expensive there." She'd asked me to advance her money a few times, which I'd been happy to do until she told me what it was for.

"He could always get a job."

"But then when would he practice?"

"At night."

"Well, he's pretty sure he'll be getting a record contract one of these days. Then he'll pay me back. And he looks so cool when he dresses like the Beach Boys."

"That's another problem, Jamie. The surfer thing. He's from Iowa. We don't have many oceans here."

The phone rang. There's a black one on her desk and a black one on mine. She smiled like a child about to do something to impress a parent. She lifted the receiver, put it to her ear and said, "Law office." Then she cringed and made a face. "The *McCain* law office." She gave me one of her embarrassed heartbreaking smiles by way of apology and waggled the phone at me. She hadn't asked the caller's name or the reason for calling, but at least I didn't have to worry about her forgetting to write down the information. I was here to write it down myself.

"This is Sam McCain."

"Where the hell are you, Sam?" Kenny Thibodeau said.

"What're you talking about?"

41

"Bennett. Somebody killed him last night. I'm out here now. I left a message with Jamie and —" Pause. "She must've forgotten."

"I'm on my way."

Jamie had begun typing with two fingers. When she'd started, she'd only used one. I'm pretty sure that's what they mean by progress.

Police Chief Clifford Sykes, Jr. once told a newspaper reporter that "fingerprints weren't all that useful when you come right down to it." He said that because he and a pair of his crack deputies had failed to dust for prints before letting the press and the neighbors walk all over a crime scene. Cliffie could not conduct a single investigation without destroying evidence. While that was bad for jurisprudence, it was great for Judge Whitney, whose family power had been ripped away by Clifford Sykes, Sr. She was always glad to see the Sykes clan humiliate and debase themselves.

The Bennett estate was one of those places people liked to drive by just for a look and a daydream. The three-story manor house and the white-fenced fiercely green pasture where their prize horses ran were something out of a painting of old

Kentucky when slaves knew their place and the master walked the grounds with a riding crop in one hand and a long-barreled Navy revolver in the other.

The drive was filled with three police cars, an ambulance, and the yellow Caddy convertible of the county medical examiner, who went by the name of Harry Sykes, if that last name tells you anything.

Kenny's black Harley was parked next to the gated entrance. I pulled off the gravel road, parked, and walked up to him. It was just now nine thirty and the temperature was eighty-four.

"I see Jamie came through for you again, huh? She forgot to tell you I called."

"Isn't her fault. She's having trouble with Turk."

"Yeah, I shouldn't have said that. Jamie's my buddy."

"She needs to lose him. Fast." I nodded to the estate. "What happened?"

"Your friend Molly was here and got the basic details and headed back to write it for the paper. I guess Linda got up this morning and couldn't find her old man in the house. She said that he walked the grounds at night when he couldn't sleep, but when she went looking for him she found him out on the far side of the pavilion. Somebody'd stabbed him twice in the neck and once in the back."

"She say anything about suspects?"

"No. And neither did William Hughes. He was headed into town. He said what Linda did, that the old man liked to walk the grounds at night. He looked shook up. I've never seen him like that."

Bennett had served in two wars, the big one as well as Korea. As a captain during the Inchon landing, one of the most decisive battles of the Korean conflict, he'd saved the wounded William Hughes's life by dragging him to safety and being shot twice in the chest while doing it. Hughes became Bennett's assistant after the war. The man ran his errands, drove for him when Bennett didn't want to slide behind the wheel, and served as an informal secretary. Bennett was known to pay Hughes very well and treat him respectfully, which was surprising because there were few others he treated that way. It was especially surprising because Hughes was a Negro.

"He said Cliffie's decided that Doran killed him. I guess they had some kind of run-in last night."

"I know they did, Kenny. I was there."

"No, I mean afterward. In front of the Royale. After Bennett left the hospital he seemed a lot calmer. Then he went to the bar in the Royale and had some drinks. When he came out he saw Doran across the street. He ran over there and they got into an argument and Bennett punched him."

I kept thinking of Lou Bennett coming apart over his son last night at the peace rally. Then I thought about how bad this looked for Doran.

As Kenny talked, I watched one of Cliffie's deputies walking down the long drive toward us. This was Bill Tomlin. He was no genius, but at least he knew that fingerprints mattered.

He walked up to us and said, "Morning, men." He was all khaki and campaign hat, playing his part in Cliffie's Western fantasy. Pancho Villa would be swooping down on us very soon now. "I'm kind of embarrassed about this — I mean you're standing on public land — but the chief wants you both to leave."

"What the hell, Bill," I said. "Public land, like you said. He can't make us move."

He had a moon face and a moon belly. His armpits and parts of his sleeves were dark with sweat. He glanced over his shoulder as if all-knowing Cliffie might be listening. "You know how it is. He ain't got a real good track record with you. With murders

45

and everything. You and the judge are always right and he's always wrong. I guess it makes him nervous that you're anywhere in the vicinity."

"Tell Cliffie for me he's a moron," Kenny said.

Tomlin smiled. "I'll let you tell him that yourself."

"Aw, forget it, Kenny. C'mon. I've got work to do, and so do you."

"I'd appreciate it, McCain," Tomlin said.

"But do me a favor, Bill."

"Sure, McCain."

"Tell him to go to hell."

4

She hadn't lost her touch with the rubber bands. Ever since she'd hired me, Judge Esme Anne Whitney would sit on the edge of her desk and fire them at me. Up until a few years ago, she would have been partaking of brandy while she did this; but a trip to a Minnesota clinic where alcoholics were treated had taught her — despite all her noisy bitter initial objections to the truth — that she was an alcoholic and had to give up drinking completely.

This morning she wore a tan linen suit, yellow blouse, tan hose, and brown pumps. The imperious and finely wrought beauty was remarkably intact, the short silver hair only adding to the appeal. And the other important things were intact, too — her endless self-regard, her impatience, and her judgment that at sixty-some years of age, who knew how to run the world better than she did?

"You look funny with a rubber band hanging off your nose."

"Gosh, and just think. Next year you'll be in *fifth* grade."

"I have a Polaroid camera in my desk, but I suppose the rubber band would fall off by the time I got it."

"Aw, shucks." I ripped the rubber band off my nose, strung it between thumb and forefinger, and fired it back at her. I missed, as I usually do.

"Now who's being juvenile, McCain?" She lifted her blue package of Gauloises from her desk and lighted one with a fey little solid silver lighter. "Lou Bennett was a friend of mine. Of sorts."

The way sunlight angled through the tall windows and illuminated the framed painting of her patrician father reminded me of the day years ago when I'd brought my parents here to meet her at her request. My mother had been taken with the severe but handsome image of the patriarch. I could remember her standing in a similar stream of light.

My folks were as quiet and polite and intimidated as if the Pope had asked them to an audience. The lustrous dark wainscoting, the rich ruby carpeting you could twist an ankle in, and the magisterial walls of leather-bound books intimidated most people. That was the intention. My parents were humbled being here, of course. Not many people from the Hills got invites. They only relaxed when the judge, who'd been unusually cordial, told them she'd invited them here so that they could hear her offer me a job as her investigator. She'd even had a bottle of champagne on hand for the occasion.

"I don't find that surprising, Judge. You and Bennett had a lot in common."

"I know how you meant that, McCain, but I'd have thought you'd have respected him. He saved a colored man's life. You're always prattling on about civil rights."

"He couldn't dine out on that forever. He did one good thing in his life, but he did a lot of bad things too."

"If you mean the run-in he had with the school board, I agreed with him one hundred percent. Those two teachers had no respect for American history. The way they taught it, we were butchers and murderers when we came here from Europe."

"He wanted a whitewash. And he wanted the teachers fired."

Something shifted in her upper-class gaze. "Well, he did go a bit far, I have to admit. I'm the one who suggested that he drop the idea of firing them. Or monitoring their classes."

"You did?"

"You don't have to sound so damned surprised, McCain. I do believe in the Constitution, you know."

"*He* didn't."

She looked unhappy. "No, he didn't." Then: "He was a bit of an ass, I have to say. But I heard about him breaking down last night at that stupid rally of yours. I felt sorry for him."

"So did I. So did most of the people at the rally. Commies have feelings, too."

She ignored my comment. Instead she inhaled deeply and exhaled a blast of smoke heavy enough to tar a road. "So tell me about this Doran person Cliffie thinks killed Bennett."

She winced at his political activities but seemed pleased when I mentioned Yale. The filthy degenerate Communist troublemaker with a Yale degree wasn't quite so filthy after all.

"Why does Cliffie think Doran killed Lou?"

I told her about the fight on the sidewalk. "That's all I know right now. As I said, Cliffie didn't want me anywhere near the crime scene."

She smiled. "I'm glad we make him nervous. And we should. He's a buffoon."

"He was a friend of Bennett's too, remember? I'm surprised the three of you didn't sit around getting drunk and making lists of all the Commies here in Black River Falls."

"I'd call you insolent if you weren't so juvenile." She left the perch on her desk and walked over to one of the windows. Good gams and a tight backside. Every one of her four husbands had no doubt been most appreciative of these and her many other charms. "Well, hop to it, McCain. I want to really humiliate Cliffie this time. Giving that stupid minister a permit for that record-burning tomorrow was the last straw."

The record-burning she had alluded to was the brainstorm of Reverend H. Dobson Cartwright, DD, which allegedly stood for Doctor of Divinity. Kenny called him Reverend Cartwright, DDT. That was more appropriate. Cartwright had a radio show and a flock and was given to publicity stunts that embarrassed everybody but true believers. Tomorrow his flock would be burning the Beatles, the Rolling Stones, and many others.

Knowing I was being dismissed, I stood up and took my last shot, "Gee, you mean you're not taking in your Lawrence Welk

51

records?"

"Good-bye, McCain."

"Jerry Vale?"

"I said good-bye."

"Kate Smith?"

She'd never given me the finger before. She looked sort of cute doing it.

5

Molly Weaver was leaning against my red Ford ragtop when I reached the parking lot behind the county courthouse. In her yellow shirtdress and tortoiseshell glasses, she gave the impression of remaining crisp on this sultry day. But the small face was anything but crisp. Dark circles under the eyes and way too much makeup. I'd never seen her like this before.

"I suppose you're mad at me."

"Hell, no, Molly. Not after I thought about it." I pulled my keys from my pocket and walked around to the driver's side. She followed me. "We were just friends. You didn't owe me anything."

"Well, I think we were a little more than friends, McCain. We *slept* together." Her words were apparently heard by an elderly couple emerging from a tugboat-sized Chrysler. Their heads whipped around as if Jesus had called them.

"Talk a little lower," I whispered.

"Well, it's true, we did sleep together." A much quieter Molly now.

I took her arm. "Look, Molly. You'd been dumped and I'd been dumped. We used each other to get through the worst of it. It was kind of like taking medicine. But we both knew that as soon as we found people we really wanted to go after, it'd be over between us. You found Doran."

That was when she broke down and fell into my arms, sobbing. "He didn't kill anybody, McCain! He really didn't!"

The elderly couple had just about made it to the courthouse, but Molly's cries stopped them. They turned around and stood there watching us. This was a lot better than daytime TV any day.

I got the door opened and guided her into the seat. I pushed her over to the passenger side, then got in myself. I punched open the glove compartment and took out a small box of Kleenex, which I placed on her lap. She was at the eye-dabbing and nose-blowing stage, the eruption being over.

"Cliffie thinks he killed Lou Bennett."

"Cliffie's a moron."

"Yes, but he's the chief of police."

"Does he have any evidence?"

"Somebody saw him in front of Bennett's

place about three o'clock this morning."

Because Molly's natural inclination was to look on the bleak side of things — Jean-Paul Sartre was a game-show host compared to her — I'd assumed that Cliffie had made his usual mistake of grabbing at the obvious. But a witness seeing Doran there was serious.

"I love him, McCain. I love him." She started crying again. I waggled the Kleenex box under her chin. She plucked one like a dandelion and put it to her jaunty little nose. But praise the Lord, it was a false start. The tears didn't get out of the gate. She just snuffled some and then went on talking. "I want to marry him. He's the man I've been waiting for all my life."

It would have been downright mean to point out that she was only twenty-two.

"Well, he needs a good lawyer, and with his money he won't have any trouble getting one, Molly."

I waved to a few courthouse employees as they passed by. One of the males gave me a smile and then the high sign. Yes, that's right. I was going to hump Molly right here in the parking lot. She faced the wall. She hadn't seen him.

Now she angled in her seat and said, "Do you have a cigarette?"

"Sure."

I lighted two and gave her one.

"I wish you smoked filters. I always get tobacco in my teeth from these."

"I'm sorry. From now on it's filters for me. Filters, filters, filters." Usually she would have smiled. Not this time.

"I have to tell you something."

"You can't be pregnant. Last night was your first time with him."

No smile this time, either.

"You know how he said he knows Joan Baez and Norman Mailer and he went to Yale?"

"Uh-huh."

"He made it up."

"Aw, shit." I didn't say that to her; I said it to myself. Of course he made it all up. All the theatricality, all the name-dropping, all the James Dean rebel stuff. He made it up. Of course. And I hadn't figured it out. Molly had had to tell me.

"He got real drunk last night and told me everything."

"Was this before or after you slept with him?"

"How do you know I slept with him?"

"Please."

"*After* I slept with him, I guess."

"Figures."

"But now I love him more than ever."

"Of course you do."

"He's had to pretend to be someone else for so many years. I feel so sorry for him."

"Me, too. I'll probably have to start using those Kleenex myself."

"Now you're being mean. He may have made things up, but he's brilliant and he's sweet and he really is against the war."

There was nothing I could say. There were women who'd loved Rasputin. There were women who'd loved Hitler. There were even women who loved Dick Nixon, Judge Esme Anne Whitney being one of them.

"He needs a lawyer. And don't say no, McCain. You'd be letting down the cause."

"What cause?"

"The *anti-war* cause. It's like Harrison said, we're all soldiers in the anti-war cause."

I sank back in my seat. Soldiers in the anti-war cause. That sounded like something good old Doran would say. "There are plenty of other lawyers in this town."

"He doesn't have any money, and the other lawyers won't help him because they don't want to be associated with our cause."

"Gee, couldn't he just call Joan Baez or Norman Mailer to help him out?"

"That isn't very funny. His whole life is at

57

stake here." Then: "Will you at least talk to him? Please, McCain? Please?"

She was right about the other lawyers in town. Nobody'd go near Mr. Wonderful. And not just because of their reputations. This was a conservative town. They really believed that people like Doran were subversives. And they threw me in for good measure.

"Please," Molly said. And for the first time, she smiled. "You know you're going to say yes eventually, so why don't you just get it over with?"

I looked at her and shook my head. "But I'm not going to start smoking filters."

"That's fine."

"And I'm not going to pretend that he's anything but a bullshit artist."

"That's fine too."

"And I'm going to send him a bill even if I only talk to him for ten minutes."

"Just say it, will you, McCain, for God's sake?"

"Shit," I said. "Yeah, I'll see the bastard."

"I knew you would." She opened her door. "Now I need to get back to work. Oh, here. I almost took this with me."

And with that she handed me the much-depleted Kleenex box. At least she'd stuffed the dirty ones in her purse.

She got about five feet from my ragtop and I said, "Hey, can you give him an alibi for last night? If you were with him all night, then the eyewitness was wrong."

"Oh, God, I wish I could, but I had to go home because I knew my period would be starting."

Of course her period was starting. It fit right in with everything else.

6

The Whitman Funeral Home is where the proper people get themselves buried. Proper translates to those who can afford it. When I played Little League, which I did to please my dad, the funeral home sponsored a team, but nobody wanted to be on it. Who wanted corpses to sponsor you? We all made fourth-grade jokes about what the real funeral home logo looked like. Boris Karloff and Bela Lugosi figured prominently in our imaginary artwork.

But if you absolutely have to die, the Whitmans will give you the fanciest of send-offs. They use two hearses instead of one to lead the cars to the cemetery, and Willis Whitman, who for years has been the baritone in the barbershop quartet here, will throw in a song at graveside, the gag being that if you pay him a little more he won't sing. As I said, this is where the wealthy go. It used to be Protestant only, but over the past ten years a few Catholics have been boxed up and gift-wrapped in the Whitman basement. Papist money spends just as well as Martin Luther's. Jewish people go to Iowa City. Everybody else goes to Sweeny's. Mr. Sweeny is a Catholic and Mrs. Sweeny is a Methodist, so it's what you might call corpse-friendly to all kinds of Christians.

There was no way I was ever going to get past the various barriers Linda Raines would have put up at the mansion. I would have to try and talk to her outside of her estate. The logical place was Whitman's. They'd no doubt be making arrangements this morning. Linda's sports car would be easy to spot.

The coffee shop directly across the street from the funeral home made waiting her out tolerable. It didn't have air conditioning, but it had enough fans and open windows to cool things down several degrees. I sat at the counter until a window table opened up. I drank iced coffee and smoked cigarettes and read the *Des Moines Register*. Around ten thirty, a quick little red car driven by an elegant brunette wearing a red scarf and Jackie Kennedy sunglasses pulled into the parking lot on the side of Whitman's.

As always, she moved with pure purpose.

She'd picked up the military bearing from her old man. She was out of her car and mounting the front steps as if somebody was chasing her.

While I waited for her reappearance I thought about Molly asking me to represent Doran. He was a con. That I didn't doubt. But to have somebody associated with our peace group accused of murdering a war hero — that discredited all of us. And more important, it discredited our political position. I had to represent the bastard.

She stayed just about thirty-five minutes. She stood on the small front porch talking to Harold Whitman, Jr., fifth generation of friendly ghouls. The body language didn't tell me anything. She was as rigid as always, all those perfectly blended curves wasted by what she obviously considered finishing school propriety.

When the tip of her tan high heel reached the sidewalk I was out of the coffee shop and bolting across the street. She was in the parking lot before I reached her.

"Mrs. Raines, Mrs. Raines."

She didn't even turn around to see who was calling her. "Leave me alone."

"I need to ask you two questions."

"I told you to leave me alone." But then I'd always thought Scarlett O'Hara was an obnoxious bitch, too.

I beat her to her car, leaned against the door so she had no choice but to face me.

"Oh, God, it's you."

"I'm sorry about your father."

"I'm sure you are. That's why you had that rally. That's why you're trying to tear down everything he fought for."

"Doran didn't kill him."

"Have you ever heard of mourning, Mc-Cain? That's what I'm doing. My father has been murdered and you're attacking me in the parking lot of the funeral home. The judge is a family friend but you've always been something of a joke. A very bad one. Now get out of my way before I call the police."

"Cliffie, you mean?"

She leaned forward and punched me in the shoulder. "Get out of my way."

"I need to know if your father had any enemies. Ones who'd been giving him grief recently."

Then she cheated. Behind those shades tears began to run, streaming down her perfect cheeks to her perfect little chin. "Will you be a goddamned gentleman for once and leave me to my mourning?" She was having a difficult time talking through her tears.

"Oh, hell," I said. "I'm really sorry. I shouldn't have bothered you." Every once in awhile you're able to see yourself through somebody else's eyes. What would I be like if my father had just died and some creep was bothering me the way I was bothering her?

I reached out, unthinking, to touch her arm. She twisted away from me. "Just let me get in my car and get out of here." She was still crying.

I stood aside immediately. I opened the door for her. She eased into her seat. I tried not to notice how her skirt rode up on those fine fine legs. She backed up fast, wheeled around fast, and left fast.

That old Sam McCain magic was working just swell.

On the way back to my office, I passed by the library. Well, I'd planned to just pass by, but when I saw the small group gathered at the bottom of the steps, I pulled my ragtop over to the curb and parked. The concrete lions on either side of the staircase watched me suspiciously the way they had been since I was checking out Hardy Boys mysteries in fifth grade.

Officer Bill Tomlin had his notepad out and was talking to Trixie Easley, the chief librarian. Two or three people in the crowd were pointing to the glass doors at the top of the stairs.

COMIE! appeared in dripping red letters across the doors. Whoever had put it there wasn't going to be taking home any prizes from a spelling bee. He or she had obviously meant COMMIE. Of course it could have been intentionally misspelled to make people think an illiterate had done the work. The library had most likely been the target because Trixie Easley had been one of the main organizers of the rally.

Molly left the crowd at the bottom of the stairs and went up to the door and started snapping photographs for the paper. She managed to look brand-new despite the heat, having changed clothes again. A pink blouse and short black skirt reminded me that even if we hadn't been soul mates, we'd been body mates. When she turned back, she saw me and waved. It wasn't a happy wave. It was an urgent one.

She was breathless by the time she reached me. I leaned against a parking meter.

"Harrison'll never get a fair trial in this town, McCain."

"They have any idea who might have done this?"

"Did you hear what I said?" She was loud

enough and angry enough to win the attention of several folks standing at the bottom of the library stairs.

"Yeah, I heard. I just don't want to be reminded of who I'm trying to help."

"He's a patriot, McCain. A *real* patriot. Not like these phony bastards from the VFW who charged into the newspaper office this morning. They want the publisher to write a front-page editorial and list the names of all the people at the rally last night."

It was too hot to argue. My shirt was starting to feel glued to my back and I had to keep wiping sweat from my eyes. "Look, first of all, they have a perfect right to be mad, all right? Veterans of Foreign Wars, does that ring any bells? That means that they fought and risked their lives. Harrison didn't. I don't agree with them about Vietnam, but we have to respect what they've done. And second of all, even if they publish a list of names — which I sure as hell don't agree with — it'll look pretty much like the same people who signed that letter to the paper protesting the war."

"Meaning what exactly?"

"Meaning if somebody wants to harass us, a new list of names won't be much added help. They've got the letter we all sent to the paper. *Your* paper."

She frowned. Those freckles and that pert little nose made me want to kiss her. "Well, I suppose Harrison's right. All this will just make his book that much more dramatic."

I was able to restrain myself. I said nothing.

"He has such a beautiful soul, McCain. A Russian soul."

"Ummm."

"You're making fun of him."

" 'Ummm' isn't making fun."

"The way you say 'ummm' it is."

Trixie joined us. "Looks like somebody doesn't agree with us."

"Doesn't it bother you?"

"Sure it does, Molly. It bothers me that they did it here instead of my house. When I signed that letter in the paper, I was signing as a private citizen, not as a representative of the library. Remember, I wrote a follow-up saying that exactly, and you people published it."

"We're probably not dealing with anybody here who's real rational," I said.

"Yes," Trixie said. In an aqua-colored blouse and dark skirt, she looked trim and competent. Which is how she kept the library — trim and competent. "That's what I'm afraid of." She glanced from me to

Molly and back to me. "You two really do make a cute couple."

"I've been thinking the same thing myself," I said.

"Well, time to open the doors. Bye."

"You didn't have to agree with her, McCain. You just did that to embarrass me."

"Yeah, that's probably right."

Then she leaned her pretty head back and gave me a stricken look. She had at last identified the monster. "My God, you're still jealous of him, aren't you?"

"Not really. I just think you're rushing into something and you may be disappointed. Believe it or not, I'm trying to be your friend."

"Some friend. There he is rotting in a dungeon, and you're out here enjoying your freedom and libeling his name to anybody who'll listen."

"Slandering."

"What?"

"You said libeling. That's written word. Slander is spoken word. You majored in journalism, remember?"

"I just can't believe you sometimes," she said, her bright blue gaze furious now. "You're just pathetic."

I started to say something, but she held up a halting hand. "Don't bother. Don't bother at all."

"I'm trying to clear him, aren't I? Not for his sake, but the sake of the cause, as he calls it. Soldiers in the anti-war movement or whatever that bullshit was."

"It wasn't bullshit. It was poetry."

I gave her an unwanted peck on the cheek and sauntered back to my ragtop.

7

Cliffie could have taken Doran in the back door of the police department, of course, but that would have disappointed the reporters he'd obviously tipped in advance. He'd even managed to snag a TV crew from one of the Cedar Rapids channels. WARNING: MAD DOG KILLER BROUGHT TO JUSTICE AT 11:35 A.M. DON'T MISS IT.

And where there were reporters, there were passersby, twenty or so of them gathered in a semicircle around the squad car from which Harrison Doran, in handcuffs, was just now emerging. I'd pushed my way to the front of the crowd, my elbows making a lot of friends in the process. Cliffie took off his campaign hat and wiped his brow with his sleeve. The temperature was ninety-two. Eight or nine cameras snapped his face, and the TV reporter said, "Did he resist arrest, Chief?"

"Oh, he tried all right." And then Cliffie

slapped his holster. "But I guess he just plain didn't know what he was up against."

At least a few of the onlookers had the grace to laugh. Most of us quit playing cowboys about age seven or so. Somebody really should point that out to Cliffie sometime. But then if he was secretly Glenn Ford, I had to admit that I was still secretly Robert Ryan. Though Ryan was taller, better looking, tougher, and smarter than me, I could definitely see a similarity between us even if nobody else could.

Doran was gray. His blue eyes were frantic. I could see that he'd been crying. Then I remembered Molly saying that he'd been drunk. Maybe what I was seeing was a combination of terror and hangover. His jeans had grass stains all over the knees, and his T-shirt was smudged in three different places with what was obviously blood. The shirt should have been taken off him and put into an evidence bag. But after all, it was Cliffie in charge, wasn't it?

Doran moved at an angle to me. I saw a long gash on the inside of his left arm. That could explain the blood on his T-shirt.

"Did you get a confession, Chief Sykes?" a reporter called out.

"Not yet. But we will."

I watched Doran's face. He didn't react in

any way. He was hiding, cowering inside himself.

"So you've got evidence against him?" another reporter asked.

"Take a look at this shirt." Cliffie turned and grabbed a handful of the T-shirt so cameras could get a clear shot of it. This was the kind of evidence you kept to yourself in an arrest. Somewhere in town, the district attorney, another member of the Sykes clan, had just fainted.

He put his campaign hat on and raised his hands. "That's it for now, everybody. We can't have the front of the police station cluttered up this way. We'll be having a press conference later this afternoon, but for now everybody should get back to what they were doing."

The new station is two-storied red brick with wide concrete steps leading to double glass doors. Cliffie likes to stand on top of the steps for his press conferences. I'm sure it makes him feel like a big-city cop.

"Now, c'mon, everybody, let's break it up."

I stood where I was as everybody else broke for their cars or back to the sidewalks.

I stepped forward. "Sykes."

I'd been speaking to his back. But when he heard my voice, he spun around so fast I thought he might draw on me. He had a sneer all ready. "Well, well, well. It's my old friend McCain. I guess I must have missed seeing you in the crowd. Being's you're so short and all."

"I'm going to be his attorney."

"Did you hear that, Doran? Sam Mc-Cain's going to be your attorney. Now you've *really* got trouble." His deputy thought this was hilarious. Doran's stunned look didn't change.

"I need to talk to him."

"Well, isn't that nice? I'll tell you what, McCain. You come back here around the same time tomorrow and I'll see what I can do for you. How's that?"

"Even you know better than that, Sykes. I don't want him questioned unless I'm present." I looked at Doran. "Do you hear that? You don't say a word unless I'm with you, all right?"

"Well now, if he should just break down and tell me about how he killed poor Lou Bennett, you sure wouldn't expect me not to listen to him, would you?"

He took Doran's arm hard enough to make him wince. Then he shoved him forward. He started walking him up the steps, then turned back to me. "You'll see him when I tell you you *can* see him, McCain, and not until then."

73

He dragged Doran up the stairs and disappeared inside.

8

The barbershop was open. I stood at the window looking in. I knew all five of the customers as well as I knew the two barbers. They were looking right back at me. Usually one or two of them would have waved and smiled. There was none of that today. I was a pariah. There was another shop a block down. I thought about going there, and then I thought the hell with it. I'd been coming here since my boyhood, but the original barbers had retired.

By the time I crossed the threshold, the men in the customer chairs had made a point of reading. The two men under the striped covers got busy talking to Mike and Earle, their respective barbers. The Amish up the highway called it shunning, after someone went against the will of the tribe.

I sat down and lighted a cigarette and picked up one of those adventure-type magazines Kenny wrote for. "Forced Into

Prostitution by Nazi Commandos!" seemed the most promising, at least judging by the illustration of an Amazonian beauty whose clothes were in tatters. Fortunately for her, she had a Bowie knife in her teeth and an Army .45 in her hand. She also had an all-American towhead in similarly tattered khaki clothes pointing a submachine gun at the Nazi commandos pouring over a nearby hill.

Usually there was conversation. The snip of scissors, the hum of the electric razor, the squeak of the barber chair as it turned — these were the only sounds. The few things I could enjoy now were the familiar smell of the shop itself, the hot shaving soap, the talc, and the aftershave.

The door opened. When I looked up, I saw Ralph DePaul walk in. He was the retired fire chief, a gray-haired man in good condition who always looked ready for a golf game. After giving up the chief's job, he ran for mayor. Local politics leaned Republican, but moderate Republican. DePaul was a Barry Goldwater man and a John Birch Society member. Some people were frightened by his thunderous speeches; others, the majority, just thought he was kind of silly, especially when he started in on his "Communists Among Us" speech.

"Well, McCain, I suppose you're proud of yourself." There were no empty chairs he could sit in. This served his purpose. He preferred to loom over me. This wasn't our first run-in. As a Republican who thought Ike was too soft, he'd tangled with me many times before.

"Free country, in case you hadn't noticed."

"Yes, and you know who made it free? The men who fought the wars. If I had a son over there and I saw you and the rest of that left-wing trash running our country down, you know what I'd do?"

"Give one of your moronic speeches?"

"Hey," Earle the barber said. "I cut hair here. I don't referee fights."

"Well, I don't blame Ralph one bit," said Larry Bellamy, a vice president at the town's largest bank. "I was in Korea. I fought and risked my life. Why shouldn't these kids do the same?"

"And anyway, Lou Bennett might be alive if he hadn't done the right thing and tried to stop that meeting. That goddamn loud-mouth punk Cliffie's got in jail — I hear you're his lawyer." Byron Davies was the city auditor. Because the barbershop was close to the courthouse and city hall, it was a gathering place for those who imagined themselves to be in power. Reputations were made and broken here. And newcomers had to pass the inspection of these men or they'd have serious problems getting set up for business.

Earle finished with his customer. The man stood up, extracted his wallet from his back pocket, and paid Earle, flourishing a final bill and saying, "That's a little extra for you." He intoned this as if he was handing him a pirate's treasure. All he got for his trouble was a little nod of the head from Earle. Everybody tipped the barbers here. It wasn't anything CBS was going to cover. As the next man moved up to the empty chair, Earle snapped the barber cape a couple of times to get rid of the hair and then hitched up his pants, ready for his next customer.

DePaul was forced to sit next to me. He picked up the *Des Moines Register,* the state paper the right always criticized as left-wing. He started going through it and said, "They only covered your little rally on page three, McCain. I guess you didn't get the publicity you wanted."

I didn't say anything. There wasn't anything *to* say. I just went on with my reading about large-breasted Nazi slaves who were being saved by the sweaty murder-crazed Yank who would soon enough be sampling them all.

"Look at this one, this picture of Berkeley. It's sickening. These are supposed to be college students. But all they do is demonstrate and complain. They got rid of the loyalty oath at that university and they're still not satisfied."

He was baiting me, and everybody in the shop knew it. Even the barbers showed the tension. Mike frowned and Earle sighed. The students had succeeded in getting rid of the loyalty oath that dated back to the days of Joe McCarthy and the House Un-American Activities Committee. Swearing loyalty to the country as part of your admissions process was decidedly Un-American in itself.

I stopped reading. I knew it wouldn't do any good to start in on him with politics. I was outnumbered.

Everybody sat in silence until the phone rang. Earle and Mike had trained us to be quiet while they were taking calls. In their past lives they'd been prison guards. The only exceptions were the Saturday afternoons when the Hawkeyes played football. They played the radio so loud, it didn't matter if you kept talking. It also didn't matter who called. The radio was never turned down. "Who's this? The Pope who?"

The call was for DePaul. "I suppose my wife wants me to get something from the store for her." He made a sour face and shook his head. He apparently hadn't signed on for errands.

He took the phone from Earle and said, "Hello." His expression changed from annoyance to wariness. He glanced around as if he was afraid one of us knew what the call was about. His fingers gripped the receiver so tightly, they were bloodless. "Uh, huh. Well, we'll have to talk about this later. Obviously." His blue eyes still continued to flick from face to face. Only a couple of us were interested. The rest read. The barbers barbered. Then he said, his voice tight and angry, "I said later. Now good-bye." He didn't hand the receiver to Earle. He walked it back to the phone himself. You could see him overcoming the urge to slam the receiver down so hard it would smash the phone into chunks of black. Then he turned and said to all of us, "Damned insurance men. They won't leave you alone anywhere."

His line didn't work for me, but it did for Mike the barber and the man in his chair. They started on a marathon of insurance-man horror stories. A few of them even sounded true.

When my turn came to be shorn, I spent

a good share of my time in the chair watching DePaul. The gaze was distracted now, the lips puckered in pique. At least he wasn't in his judgmental mood. He was manly enough, I suppose, but there was a scold in him too, the maiden aunt who thought all little boys were naughty and all little girls were fools to associate with anybody who had a penis.

Then he surprised me. He slapped down the magazine he'd been holding and not reading and stood up. "Earle, I guess I'll have to take a rain check. I just remembered an appointment I have in fifteen minutes."

"Hell, Ralph, that's too bad. Stop back. Things'll probably slow down in an hour or so."

He said good-bye to everybody but me and then left. His sudden exit had made the call he'd gotten much more mysterious.

9

The heat would likely kill somebody today. An elderly person probably, one of those who get overlooked by everybody and are found dead a few days later by the mailman when the smell gets bad. By the time I was halfway back to my ragtop, my white short-sleeved shirt was soaked. I walked under awnings as often as I could. And that was how I almost literally bumped into William Hughes. He came fast out of Flanagan's Pharmacy just as I was crossing past the entrance. He jerked to a stop and said, "Sorry."

I was moving pretty fast myself and probably wouldn't have noticed him if he hadn't said anything. William — never "Will" — Hughes was a tall, thin, gray-haired man in his late fifties. His handsome dark face is dominated by brown eyes that don't merely look at you. They judge you. The tautness of the gaze extends to the tautness of the entire body, as if he's always prepared for the worst. It's a defensive posture. Right now he showed no sadness or anger for the loss of his friend and boss, but then he wouldn't. Not publicly, anyway. He wore a deep-blue golf shirt, light-blue well-creased slacks, and a pair of black loafers that he'd shined with military fervor. He wore a spicy aftershave. He didn't look at all happy to see me.

"You have a few minutes, William?"

"I'm really in a hurry to get back to Linda. You know what happened, don't you?"

"That's what I want to talk to you about."

We had to move to let people in and out of the pharmacy entrance. Hughes had a small white prescription sack in his large right hand and started tapping it against his leg. "I'm really in a hurry."

"I'm representing Harrison Doran."

The eyes narrowed and a frown creased his mouth. "Then I probably shouldn't be talking to you."

"I can always subpoena you."

The smile was cold. "You can always try." A deep sigh and then: "I really am in a hurry, McCain. And if it's a question about what happened, you already know the answer. Your man killed Colonel Bennett."

"You're sure of that?"

"A witness put him out in front of our place at three A.M."

"What the hell was a witness doing out there at that time?"

This time the smile was one of satisfaction. He was about to nail my ass to the wall. "The kind of witness who'd been at the hospital most of the night waiting for his wife to have a baby. He stayed with her for two hours after the delivery and then drove on home. He passes by our house every night. And he made a positive identification of Doran."

"What's his name?"

He tapped me on the chest with the prescription sack. "Isn't that what your private investigator's license is for, McCain?"

Wendy Bennett's house was a split-level ranch situated on a rise overlooking a clear blue turn of river. The silver Mercury sedan in the drive, the powerful TV antenna on the roof, and the ruthlessly kept lawn and garden spoke of solid middle-class prosperity. Nothing arrogant, but nothing humble either.

She sat on the front steps smoking a cigarette and watching me walk toward her. We'd been friends in high school. Even though she'd been a cheerleader and the daughter of wealth, Wendy McKay had been forced to sit next to me in homeroom and various other school functions because of the Mc's in our names. That was how she'd treated me at first, anyway. Forced confinement. But eventually we started talking. I'd made her laugh. Later on, I'd come across Andrew Marvell's line from the fifteenth century: "The maid who laughs is half taken." I'd never taken the blonde, green-eyed girl with the body that occasionally made standing up embarrassing, but we did become friends.

She wore a peasant skirt and a white blouse, and her shining blonde hair was in a ponytail. I sat down next to her and looked at the timberland on the other side of the road. The location was just about perfect, a sense of isolation but only five minutes away from town.

I'd called earlier and asked if I could come out and talk to her. I'd been surprised that she'd been home and not at the Bennett mansion. I was even more surprised that she'd agreed to see me. She smelled of heat and perfume, a mixture that stirred me.

"Thanks for coming out."

"Thanks?"

"Yes. It gave me an excuse to get out of

85

there. Linda wanted me to stay but that place always suffocates me. I told her an old friend of mine was in town and I had to meet her for lunch. She didn't like it, but she doesn't like much I've ever done anyway."

Linda Raines was Wendy's sister-in-law, Wendy having married Bryce a few years before he'd gone to Vietnam.

"Was it always like that?"

She smiled. She had teeth so white, you wanted to lick them. "To her I'll always be 'the cheerleader.' Her father used to tease me about it and I think she was jealous. She caught him sort of patting my bottom one night when he was drunk. I got the feeling that she wanted him to save that for her." The smile was impish now. "Pretty bitchy, huh?"

"Didn't Bryce ever say anything to her?"

"Oh, no, Bryce wouldn't. They had this strange relationship. They never criticized each other."

"Seriously?"

"Very seriously." She put her hand on mine. "Thanks for coming up at Bryce's funeral. You said just the right thing."

"I did?"

"Yes, because you didn't say anything. Not with words. But with your eyes. And you held my hand just the right way and I thought of all the times you made me laugh in high school, and for just a minute there I didn't have to think of how I wasn't Bryce's first choice."

"First choice for what?"

"For wife material."

"I'm not following you."

"Karen Shanlon? From high school? The really pretty red-haired girl with the limp?"

"But they broke up when he went to college."

Her ponytail wagged. "That's what everybody thought. But he kept in touch with her and he managed to come home once a month or so. That's why he went to Northwestern. He could drive home. The only reason he finally broke it off was because of his father. But then Lou figured out he was seeing her on the sly anyway."

"I see her sister Lynn all the time. She works in the courthouse. Very quiet and very pretty. But I guess I haven't thought of Karen in a long time."

"Well, Bryce didn't have that problem. He thought of her a lot." She leaned back with her palms flat against the entranceway. I tried not to notice how her breasts were defined by the material of her blouse. "That's why he went into the Army."

Now I knew why she'd agreed to my visit. She needed to go to confession. Lou's murder had forced her to face her life with the Bennetts.

"She died in that fire and he couldn't handle it. He used to try and hide it from me, Sam. You know, how he felt about her. But after she died — He just had to get away from everything. Even a war was better than staying around here without her. That fire really took its toll. And the whole thing struck me as odd, the way she died, I mean. She was supposedly smoking in bed and it went up. Bryce said she rarely smoked, maybe three or four times a year when they'd be out somewhere. He seemed upset about the report they did on the fire, too. The whole thing just tore him apart."

"Did he see her while you were married?"

"That's the funny thing. I'm not sure. Whenever I'd start in on him about her, he'd tell me how sorry he was. That he should have told me about her before I agreed to marry him." She sat up again, this time with her elbows on her knees, her chin on her hands like a little girl staring out a summer window on a rainy day. "He tried to be honorable about it. He even said that that's why we shouldn't have kids until he'd worked through it. And he was even worse after she died. That's when he let Lou find him a spot where it was guaranteed he'd go to Vietnam."

Listening to her, watching her, I realized that in all the years I'd known her, I hadn't known her at all. She was smiles and laughter and breasts and perfect ankles, but emotionally she wasn't real in any sense, because I'd never seen her hurt. I'd always supposed that with her looks and her money, she was one of those gleaming girls whose worst tragedy would be losing her looks at sixty or so.

"I'll bet you didn't expect this when I said you could come out here." She strained a smile for my sake.

"I'm just sorry you've gone through all this."

"You know — so am I. But I can't hate him. I can resent him, but I can't hate him. I blame Lou and Linda for breaking Bryce and Karen up. They should have stayed together."

"That would have left you out. You obviously loved him."

"Boy, did I," she said wistfully. "I'd get kind of woozy sometimes just seeing him walking toward me. It was like being drunk. Sometimes I resented it. You know how it is? When someone has that much power

89

over you?"

"Sure."

"So it's happened to you?"

"Two or three times."

"The funny thing was, Bryce was never that way about me. But I'm sure he was about Karen. He had this little metal box that he kept in the garage with his tools. A pretty good hiding place if I hadn't been looking for a screwdriver one day. I saw the box there and it looked wrong. Just out of place. So I took it down and opened it and I thought I'd pass out. I really did. I had to keep my hand against the wall to hold myself up. I managed to get to the steps of the back porch. I sat down there and opened the box again and started looking through all the photos of her he had. Her whole life. Teeny-tiny baby pictures right up through high school. Now, that's love. Caring about somebody that way. I don't think I've ever been hurt like that in my life. But I hurt myself. He'd hidden the photos from me. He had to know what they'd do to me if I ever saw them."

"Did you ever ask him about them?"

"Oh, no. How could I? But I never quite got over them. I still think about them three or four times a day. Sometimes I want to take a knife and cut that part of my brain out. It probably doesn't take up much space up there. Just slice out that one little part, the part about that little metal box."

I'd been thinking the same thing about Jane since she'd left. Some freak accident that would magically cleave away all memory of her but leave everything else intact.

"I was such a bitch in high school. Sometimes I think this is just me getting what I deserve."

She had a small soft laugh. "*Nobody* was as bad as Diane. You remember what she wrote in the yearbook about what she planned to do after graduation? 'I plan to become a goddess.' She was only half kidding."

There was a breeze. I wanted to close my eyes and ride it. It made me realize how comfortable I felt sitting here with Wendy. That had been something neither Molly nor I had ever felt with each other. The simple pleasure of just hanging out together. We'd been all jittery with the need to talk about being dumped and then to have vengeance sex as balm for our wounds. One of Kenny's best serious stories was called "Grudge Humping on the Amazon." He'd gone through the same thing himself.

Inside, the phone rang. "That'll be Linda.

She keeps calling and telling me to come back. According to her, my proper place is in the mansion." She pushed up, dusting off her bottom with finely turned hands. She sighed and shook her head. "Maybe I'm just being a bitch. Maybe I'd better take it."

I stood up and she took my hand. "Thanks for coming out, Sam. I really needed to talk to someone."

And then what I'd always wanted to happen, happened. She kissed me on the mouth and then took me to her. I had to imagine myself wearing an invisible pair of handcuffs, otherwise I'd do something very foolish.

"All right," she said as we broke apart, nagging at the nagging phone. "I'm coming, I'm coming."

Then she was inside and I was walking to my car.

10

In the lobby of the new police station, you can find three large framed photographs. One is of our governor, which is only fitting, while the other two bear a remarkable resemblance to Cliffie himself. In fact, they *are* of Cliffie. Both show him in his khaki uniform and campaign hat. One of them depicts him in a crouch aiming his Magnum right at the viewer. It's a pulp-magazine cover pose. The other shows Cliffie standing next to the gallows where prisoners were hanged. The picture remained even after the legislature voted against capital punishment a few months ago. Cliffie didn't want to deprive his fans of any thrills.

The woman at the front desk was Marjorie Kincaid, a buxom middle-aged woman with a tinted black beehive hairdo and a sweet, somewhat mannish face. She was supposed to hate me — that was an official order in this department — but if nobody was looking she always had a quick grin for me. Marjorie and my mom had been friends in school.

"How's your dad?"

"Not very well, Marjorie."

"I always told your mom she got the best one. We used to double-date all the time. I got Hank." She made a face. "He fell off the wagon again last month."

"I'm sorry, Marjorie."

"I know it's not his fault. I went through that program with him, where they teach you that it's a disease and everything. But that doesn't make it any easier."

"Well, why don't you serve him some coffee and then you two can really get cozy?" A familiar and unwelcome voice.

There are times when I think Cliffie has superpowers. He can just appear, like one of those invisible avengers who can pop in and out of visibility in comic books.

Marjorie swiveled in her chair and started typing. Maybe I'd have Jamie come over here and get a few lessons.

"I'd like to see Harrison Doran."

"No can do, McCain. I told you it'd be at least tomorrow."

"I take it you haven't talked to your cousin."

"What cousin?"

94

"Your cousin the district attorney?"

"What about him?"

"I called him about twenty minutes ago. He said you *have* to let me see him. By law."

"Bullroar." Cliffie always watched his language in the presence of a woman.

"Go call him."

His face was flushed now. He was so mad I wondered if his campaign hat would start spinning around on his head. "You wait here."

I knew better than to talk any more to Marjorie. I went over and sat on one of the new scotch-plaid couches and smoked a cigarette.

An attorney named Dix Tolliver came in and nodded at me. He looked as if he'd just spotted a pile of doggie excrement. He was one of the Brahmins, a second-generation Brahmin in fact. He always dressed as if he was about to appear before the Supreme Court. I wondered how many gray flannel suits he owned. While he waited for Marjorie to finish up her phone call, he said, "So I guess that whole story about Doran being a rich boy from Yale isn't true?" The patrician nose sniffed the plebian air. "And he already had a warrant out for his arrest back East?"

I tried not to look surprised. I didn't want to give him the satisfaction of knowing that

95

he knew something vital about my client that I didn't know. And saying anything could be dangerous. If, for instance, I said, "Yeah, but it's a minor matter" and he said, "You mean killing a family of six is a minor matter?" where would I be then?

Fortunately, Marjorie hung up and distracted him. He was here to see a detective on another matter. She spoke into an intercom and before you could say kiss my ass a detective appeared. The men shook hands and joked a bit like the golfing buddies they were and then disappeared into the innards of the station. Face it. I was just jealous I didn't get that kind of treatment.

Cliffie would be damned if he debased himself by telling me that I had the legal right to see Doran. He sent a uniformed cop named Winslow to guide me back to one of the interrogation rooms.

"I assume you've got the room bugged?"

"That supposed to be funny?" Winslow, all khaki and malice, said as he scratched at his cheek as we moved along the hallway. He had a boozer's nose.

He opened the door for me then stood aside to let me pass. A long narrow room with a long narrow folding table and six folding chairs and several cheap chipped glass ashtrays. Woolworth specials. Despite the air conditioning, the room smelled of used old sad griefs.

"We'll bring him in. You have fifteen minutes."

"The DA said I have half an hour."

"Around here, the chief makes the rules." He made sure to slam the door.

Harrison Doran looked five years older when Winslow followed him into the room. The leg irons and the handcuffs clanked and clinked. His expression was mournful. His jail suit was gray and two sizes too big for him. Winslow slammed him into a chair. Doran's eyes were downcast. He hadn't looked at me once.

"Fifteen minutes." He managed to slam the door even harder this time.

"We don't have much time." His head still hung down, his long, lanky blond hair covering his forehead. "Did you hear me, Doran? We don't have much time."

The eyes were crazed when I finally saw them. "I wanted a real lawyer. I know who you are, man. I need a real lawyer. I mean I don't mean any offense, but when I heard you tell Sykes you were my lawyer, I couldn't believe it. Molly said she'd help me, but —" His shrug reinforced his words. "I need a major lawyer."

"The kind Joan Baez could get you?"

97

"You can kiss my ass, you hack."

I stood up. "Okay, moron. I just paid my dues. Be sure and mention that to Molly."

"Molly. She's an idiot."

I wondered what kind of sentence I'd get for picking up one of the folding chairs and beating him about the head sixty or seventy times.

Then he started sobbing. Everybody was crying this morning. He brought his silver-cuffed hands to his face and wept. I sat back down and smoked a cigarette. I pushed the pack across the table. When he saw it, he snuffled up some tears and said, "How am I supposed to light it?"

"Take a cigarette. I have a match."

"I didn't mean to insult you."

"Sure you did." Then I just said it. "Look, I think you're a showboat bullshit artiste and you think I'm a hayseed lawyer. Right now neither of those things matter."

He manipulated his hands around the cuffs to get a cigarette in his mouth. It was like one of those tricks contestants on game shows have to perform to win a refrigerator. I gave him a light.

"Man, you really tell it straight. 'Showboat bullshit artiste.' Wow." He was blinking at seventy miles an hour.

"Anybody hit you while you've been in here?"

"No."

"How many times did they talk to you?"

"Three times. Always with that moron Sykes. He yelled at me so much, I was surprised he had a voice left."

"What did you tell him?"

"Nothing, man. You kidding? I'm a smart guy."

"Yeah, Yale, wasn't it?" Then: "Sorry." Then: "Harrison Doran probably isn't your real name, is it?"

"No. It's Elmer Dodd."

"You're kidding me. Elmer Fudd?"

"Gee, I never heard that one before."

He exhaled smoke in a long wavering stream. "I grew up on a farm in Ohio and ran away and joined the Navy when I was sixteen. When I got out, I tried working in a grocery store, but I couldn't cut it. I just saw my whole life in front of me, you know? I couldn't deal with it." He still snuffled up tears once in a while. "So this chick I knew got me interested in this theater group — this was in New York — and I really got caught up in acting. I mean I'm good looking. That helped. But I also had a little talent." A quick smile. "That *didn't* help. Hundreds of people have a little acting talent. So I started inventing roles for myself to play in real life."

"Like Harrison Doran, political activist?"

"Yeah, it's like a drug. Pretending you're somebody else. You don't have to be you, you know what I mean? People give you places to live and feed you and you can pretty much have any girl you want. But I never had this happen before."

"There's a warrant out for your arrest in the East. What's that about?"

"I got a gig as a disk jockey in this real small station. I started banging the owner's mistress. He tried to hit me with a whiskey bottle one night. I beat the shit out of him. But he was a big man in town, so the cops put it all on me. And I ran."

A knock on the door. "Five minutes, McCain. The chief talked to the DA, and the DA said he didn't say anything about you having a half hour."

Elmer Dodd smiled. "So you like to make up stuff, too?"

Winslow went away, footsteps slapping down the hallway.

"What were you doing at Bennett's at three in the morning?"

He shook his head. "Molly'd gone home. I don't remember much; I mean I was really shit-faced, man. I took her car. I'd seen

Bennett's place before. I remember being so mad I wanted to tell him off. That's another thing I have a problem with. My temper. I've got a bad one. But then I always get depressed, too. I guess I might as well tell you."

"Tell me what?"

"There was this girl I was in love with, and she left me after she found out I was just making up my past. And I went kind of crazy. They put me in a mental hospital for three weeks. I still have a lot of trouble with depression, I guess."

I tried not to think about how the DA would characterize Elmer Fudd here: a bunco artist with a bad temper who'd spent time in a mental hospital and was seen at the murder victim's home at three in the morning. Not to mention two violent confrontations with Bennett. A lawyer's dream.

"Do you remember seeing Bennett?"

"I didn't make it that far. I remember tripping over something when I was walking up the driveway. That's how I got this gash on my arm. I must have passed out. It was about four o'clock when I woke up. I was in the same place. I obviously didn't make it up to the house."

"So you're saying you didn't kill him?"

He took a deep breath. "I'm really in

trouble, aren't I?"

This time I heard Winslow before he got to the door. The knock was louder this time. "Your five minutes is up."

"I timed it. I've got two minutes left."

"Not according to my watch." He opened the door. "C'mon, McCain. You're lucky you got to see him at all."

Elmer Dodd rose up out of his seat and reached out for me, his handcuffs clacking. "You're not going to leave me like this, are you, man?"

"I'll be back." There wasn't anything more to say. I saw the kid in him now. Scared and desperate. The tears were back.

"Get out of here, McCain." Winslow put his hand on my shoulder and I brushed it away.

"I'll bet you don't wash your hands after you go to the bathroom, do you?"

Believe it or not, some people don't find me amusing.

11

Sue had strung a clothesline from Kenny's trailer to a utility shed he'd bought prefab at Monkey Ward's. There was something timeless about her hanging clothes in the Midwestern sunlight, her fine figure in a simple blue housedress, a wooden clothespin between her teeth and their small Border collie running around and around the hanging sheets and shirts. Trixie Easley had recently collected photographs from the last century and put them in a display in the library to show the eternal work of women. She also created a section of books that disabused the John Wayne myth-seekers about who put in the most hours on the frontier. It was women, not men. When men's work was done for the day, the women worked long into the night, this after getting up earlier than the menfolk to get breakfast ready and start the day. The book I read was about women on the plains of

Kansas. There were a lot of suicides.

When she heard me coming down the dirt road that led to the big shade trees and the trailer, she stopped her work and waved at me. Pepper came out to run around my car and lead me the rest of the way. Sue and Pepper and the clothes on the line . . . how much Kenny's life had changed for the better.

Sue always had a hug for me. "Shush, Pepper," as the dog raced around and around me. Pepper was in bad need of more visitors, it seemed. All her attention focused on a single person was pretty much overwhelming. "He's inside working. He got up at dawn and started in. Fortunately I've learned how to sleep through the typing. Any special plans for Labor Day?"

The smell of the fresh wet wash was sweet on the dusty heat of the early afternoon. "Nothing planned. I'm working for Harrison Doran."

She nodded, her pretty Italian face breaking into a smile. "All last night Kenny was telling me how much you hated Doran. He called your office a while ago and talked to Jamie. She said you'd agreed to help him. Molly must have changed your mind."

"Yeah, Molly did — and Cliffie. He's already convicted Doran. And there's no other lawyer in town who'll help him."

"I have to say Doran's pretty hard to take. I sat in Burger-Quik one afternoon and listened to him tell anybody who'd listen what a cool guy he was."

"Yeah, but still —"

She kissed me on the cheek. "But you're doing the right thing. Go in and tell Kenny to rest for a while. He needs a break."

Sue had turned the small silver trailer into a home. The floor was carpeted, the furniture was new, as was the gas range and washer-dryer. And gone from the walls were the framed covers of a few of the soft-core novels Kenny had written. All that remained was the framed photograph of Jack Kerouac. Most people had Jesus on their walls, Kenny had Jack.

Kenny worked at a small oak desk pushed against the west wall. Sometimes he worked with music in the background. His taste ran to Miles Davis and John Coltrane and Hank Williams. He could type ninety words a minute perfectly. I never mentioned that to Jamie.

He usually worked nonstop. He wasn't aware of me until I was two feet from his desk and said, "I don't think there's enough sex in that scene."

He looked up, smiling. "Hey, I hear you're

working for Doran. Good, because the radio makes it sound like he's already convicted. He's an asshole, but he deserves somebody helping him."

I pointed to the paper in his typewriter. "What's this one?"

" 'Twisted Twilight.' "

"Lesbians?"

"You can't go wrong with lesbians."

"Guy comes along and rescues one of them from decadence?"

"Rance Haggarty's his name. Pro football player and world-class lover. Got a schlong that spoils women for life." He laughed. "There's some very cold Pepsi in the fridge. Why don't you get both of us one?"

"Rance as in 'rancid'?"

"I keep wanting to write a book where the lesbians end up happily together. You know I correspond with gay women who write soft-core. They're very bright nice women. Fortunately for me, they understand the market and what you have to do, so they don't hate me. But then, hell, their own books have to have the endings when one of the women goes off with a guy. Or gets hit by a train." His laugh hadn't changed in twenty-two years.

I got our Pepsis. I sat on the couch. Kenny turned his chair around so he could face me. "Time for me to pull out my deerstalker cap?"

"I really need some help. Linda Raines isn't going to help me and neither is William Hughes. I need to know who really had it in for Bennett."

"Plenty of people, from what I've always heard."

"But I need to narrow the list down."

"I can probably do that for you."

Kenny knew as much about our little town as anybody in it. He started a novel set here when he was still in high school. In doing research, he learned not only our history but also who was who and why in our own time. Despite the books he writes, most people like Kenny. They'll talk to him because his boyishness puts them at ease.

"Who're you going to talk to next?"

"Lynn Shanlon. She knows a lot about the Bennett family. I know they never accepted Karen."

"No surprise there, Sam. She came from the Hills and she had a limp. You sure wouldn't want either of those things in the blood line."

"Choate. West Point. Hyannis Port. Lou did all right for himself coming from here."

"Yeah, but only because his old man inherited a fortune when Lou was eight years old."

That was what I meant about Kenny knowing the town. "I'd forgotten that. Where'd the money come from?"

"Oil. The father's brother was a wildcatter. He was also a convicted felon. Nearly killed a man in a bar fight in Waco. Served three years. But all was forgiven when his gushers came in. Full pardon from the governor." He smiled. "You know how fast money can make you respectable. Surprised the Pope didn't make him a saint."

"What about Bennett's business partner Roy Davenport?"

"Another felon. Lou liked to walk right up to the line legally. He had a number of businesses that probably involved outright crime, including cheap cigarettes in from Canada. He needed a fixer. Davenport was his fixer for the side businesses, but he was impressive enough to meet people at the country club."

"Why'd Davenport leave Bennett?"

"A woman named Sally Crane. She was one of their secretaries. Lou hired good-looking married women who were willing to stay a little late if there were bonuses in their paychecks. Davenport started sleeping with the Crane woman on the side. Except Bennett didn't want to share her and couldn't believe that Davenport actually had feelings for her. They got into a fistfight one night and Davenport beat him up pretty badly. And that was that."

"If you hear anything more about Davenport, let me know, huh? I already owe you a good meal for what you just told me."

"I'll keep calling people, seeing what I can find out."

By the time I reached the door, Kenny had already turned back to his typewriter. By the time I reached the ground and was greeted by a hand-slurping Pepper, Kenny was punishing his typewriter at a rate poor Jamie could only dream of.

Lynn Shanlon wore a white T-shirt and red shorts. She probably caused more than one man to gawk at her as he passed by in his car. She was comely and cute as she shoved the hand mower across the sloping front yard of her small white clapboard house. If she noticed me pulling into her driveway, she didn't let on. She thrust that mower with serious intent. A buccaneer of the blades.

I stood on the edge of her lawn and waited until she'd turned back in my direction. I waved when she saw me. She didn't wave back. She mowed her way to me and then stopped, wiping sweat from her brow with the back of her arm. The displeasure in the brown eyes told me that she knew who I was and didn't like me at all.

"Wondered if I could talk to you."

Despite the wrinkles around eyes and mouth, her perfect little features would always keep an air of youth about her.

"I guess you're forgetting what you did to me, Mr. McCain."

"What are you talking about?"

"My neighbor down the block — Mrs. Hearne? — you represented her against me. She claimed that my boyfriend's dog always tore up her garden?"

"She filed the complaint against him, right? Pekins or something like that?"

"Perkins. And it was one of the reasons we broke up. I got too good a deal on this house to move, and he wouldn't live here with me without his dog."

"But the dog was tearing up her garden. She had a pretty reasonable complaint."

She sighed. Her thin arms were covered with blades of grass. She dug into the pocket of her shorts and brought out a pack of Chesterfields. She got one lighted and said, "Oh, hell, who am I kidding? We were going to break up anyway, I guess. Every time I'd bring up marriage, he'd change the subject. But that doesn't make Mrs. Hearne any less of a bitch. She would have been right at home in Salem, burning witches."

That made me laugh. "Other than that, you like her, huh?"

She had a quick girly smile. "Other than that, I'm crazy about her."

A green DeSoto convertible drove past, the male driver downright enchanted by the sight of Lynn Shanlon in her shorts. "My ex-husband was like that. Everywhere we'd go, I'd have to watch him watch every girl in the place. I thought Perkins might be different. But no. You men are all lechers." She dragged on her cigarette. "So why're you here?"

"I'd like to ask you some questions about your sister and when she was seeing Bryce Bennett."

"Does this have anything to do with Lou being killed?"

"Could have. I'm representing Harrison Doran."

She dropped her smoke to the grass, twisted it out with the sole of one of her red Keds. "You've got your hands full then. I heard Chief Sykes on the radio this morning. I'll admit he's an idiot sometimes, but Doran being out there at three in the morning —"

"Did your sister ever tell you about any of Lou Bennett's enemies? She must have spent some time out there."

"Not unless she had to. She was insecure enough with her leg, the way the poor kid limped. Her foot was run over by a car when she was four and it wasn't fixed correctly. The way the Bennetts treated her didn't exactly make her feel any better about herself." Then: "Hey, good afternoon, Dave." She trotted down the driveway to meet the mailman. "Are you ready for the weekend?" she said as he handed her the mail.

"Probably go to the parade."

"You're not going to burn any Beatles records?"

Dave laughed. "If I did, my daughters would burn *me*."

It was an afternoon of heat and lawn work and little kids cooling off with moms aiming hoses at them and teenage girls in bikinis sunning themselves on towels and hoping to put a fair number of men in mental hospitals.

When she returned, she waved a handful of envelopes at me. "Bills. Between my job at the courthouse and my big alimony check, I can almost pay these." Then: "My sister loved Bryce and Bryce loved her. His father forced him to break it off. Karen never got over it, and I don't think Bryce did either."

"Did he ever try to contact her after he was married?"

"I don't know. I was living in Chicago with my ex-husband the banker. I came back here one week before the fire in her little bungalow. I think about that all the time. I was so upset over my husband divorcing me, I didn't spend much time with her because I didn't want to bring her down with all my whining. We'd planned on spending the whole day together sometime; drive into Cedar Rapids or Iowa City. But then she died." The voice became despondent. "I loved her as much as she loved Bryce."

"I'm trying to remember the fire. Was there anything strange about it?"

"Are you kidding? Everything about it was strange. First of all, she rarely smoked. Once in a while when she was really depressed or something, she'd puff on a few cigarettes. So that bothered me. And the fact that she didn't wake up in time to get out. My sister was a very light sleeper. Very light."

"Did you talk about this to anybody?"

"To anybody who'd listen, including the mayor and the fire chief. They thought I was just distraught because my sister died. You know, that I was making things up."

"Did the Bennetts give you any kind of support?"

"You must be nuts. Why would they?"

"Well, your sister and Bryce had gone out for quite a while."

"The only one who paid any attention to Karen was Linda's husband David. He was quite taken with her, especially after he'd had a few drinks."

"She told you that?"

"She didn't have to. I got invited to the mansion a few times. I saw it for myself. He's like my ex. The grass always looks greener and everything. Linda's a bitch, but you can't take her beauty from her. And I can't blame her for hating my sister a little. Raines got serious about her. Because he couldn't have her. He has quite the ego. Wrote her a few letters even."

"Did she ever tell Bryce?"

She devastated a mosquito by slamming her palm against her forearm. "No. She was afraid what it would do to the whole family if they found out. She was afraid Lou and Linda would blame her."

She made a face. "I don't know why the hell I'm talking to you, anyway. I really am pissed about you being that old bitch's lawyer."

"One more question."

She turned a sigh into Hamlet. "Yeah? One more?"

"Did Lou have any enemies that your sister heard him talk about?"

The smile was bitter. "Lou considered everybody an enemy. People were a nuisance to him." Then: "His business partner. Or ex-business partner. Roy Davenport. They really ended up hating each other. Somebody told me they heard that Davenport beat Lou up pretty badly one time. I hope that's true." She put her hand over her eyes and squinted at me. "So you really think this Doran is innocent?"

"I do, yes. Or I wouldn't be trying to help him."

"Well, I guess you can try."

She turned the mower around and went back to work. I watched her for several long moments. Those red shorts immortalized her bottom.

12

IF YOU HAVE THE DEVIL'S MUSIC IN YOUR
HOME BRING IT HERE LABOR DAY FOR OUR
RIGHTEOUS FIRE!
— REVEREND H. DOBSON CARTWRIGHT

The sign was in black and white and strung
between two small oak trees that sat on
church property. If you were headed west
through town, as I was, you couldn't miss
it.

The Church of the Sacred Realm was a
one-story concrete building that had previ-
ously been a warehouse for an auto-parts
supplier. A thirty-foot steel cross had been
set in place on the roof. For special holy
events, Cartwright rented a spotlight to
shine on it. At least two people claimed to
have been healed by the gleaming cross. I
was surprised that athlete's foot could be
vanquished that easily.

Cartwright was a tent-show preacher no

116

matter how hard he tried to disguise it. He dressed like a banker, spoke perfect English, and never harped about money at Sunday services. The harping he left to a cadre of "Visitors," as they were called, who worked the homes of the flock. They were holy variations on Mob muscle.

Five or six times a year, he created a spectacle that got him on local and sometimes (much to the embarrassment of the Chamber of Commerce) national TV. He had burned sexy paperbacks (he never mentioned Kenny by name, but I was worried that one of his more zealous Visitors might try to burn Kenny out), chopped up Barbie dolls (scandalous attire), smashed in a brand-new 21″ Admiral TV console to demonstrate how little he cared for sinful TV, sponsored a "Good Girl" modeling contest in which the winners looked as if they were in training to become Amish, and had one of his parishioners paint a fifteen-foot-tall portrait of Elvis as the anti-Christ. Elvis's guitar was in flames, and a forked snake tongue sprang from his mouth.

Burning the Beatles was a good idea by Cartwright's standards. Some parents were leery of the group, just as many parents had been of Elvis. They'd heard the news about Carnaby Street with all its promiscuity —

my God, fashion models with their breasts exposed — and suspected the end was near. These were the parents who helped get Cartwright on TV for all his stunts. Most parents rightly considered him a joke. Grandma had had Sinatra, the parents had had Bill Haley and then Elvis, and now their kids had the British Invasion. There were plenty of other things more deserving of parental attention.

Thinking about Cartwright always made me smile. I got two or three minutes of amusement as a reward for passing by that giant steel cross.

The main drag was just now lighting up for the night. Most people had some time off to be with their friends and families. The Dairy Queen's chill white luminescence showed lines that stretched down the block. The same for the two downtown movie theaters where *The Ipcress File* with Michael Caine was up against *Help* with the Beatles, the latter probably sending the good Reverend Cartwright into suicidal depression. Little kids held strings to the red and blue and yellow and pink balloons their parents had bought them from the vendor in front of the A&P.

Elderly couples sat on bus benches, the buses having stopped running at six o'clock.

I wondered what they made of it all. Some of them had seen Saturday nights when horses and buggies had plied our Main Street. Now it was the predatory crawl of teenage boys in their cars searching for girls, me having been one of them for several years myself. I always watched for the black chopped and channeled '49 Merc, the one even cooler than James Dean's in *Rebel Without a Cause.* It was as brazen and sure of itself as only a classic car can be — it spoke of power and lust and longing; and now when I saw it pull into place with the parade of cars cruising the street, I felt better. Or maybe I just felt rational.

A breeze cooled me as I walked the final steps to the police station. I was calm now, and I wouldn't shout at Cliffie as I'd planned. I'd methodically point out to him that by not giving me adequate time with my client, he might well jeopardize the trial and give me grounds for appeal. This was unlikely as hell, but Cliffie knew even less about law than he did about police work.

The lobby area was empty. The drunks and the fistfighters would fill up the eight cells starting in a few hours, and their loved ones would be out here in the lobby pleading for them to be released. Some would be embarrassed, some would be angry, a few

— especially the women whose husbands pounded on them — would be secretly happy.

Mary Fanelli was behind the desk. Since we'd gone to grade school together, she was another one who disregarded Cliffie's Hate McCain policy.

"How's your dad, Sam?"

"Not any better. Maybe a little worse."

"We did a novena for him at the early Mass yesterday."

"Thanks, Mary. Is the chief around?"

"Softball game." She brought forth a can of 7UP and sipped it. She was a slight woman with a sharp face redeemed by sweet brown eyes. "Bill Tomlin's here. Want me to buzz him?"

"I'd appreciate it."

She got on the intercom and told Tomlin I was here. She clicked off a second too late. I heard his "Shit" loud and clear. She smiled. "He knows you're going to ask him to make a decision, and he hates making decisions. You know how the chief is. We all hate decisions because no matter what we do, it's wrong according to him."

Tomlin walked toward me as if he was expecting to be executed. "Chief's not here."

"That's what Mary said. I'd like to see Harrison Doran."

"Aw, shit, McCain, c'mon. You really want to put my tit in a wringer like that? No offense, Mary." Mary grinned.

"I'm going to make it easy for you, Bill. I got permission from the DA to see Doran for half an hour. Your boss kicked me out after fifteen minutes. That means I'm owed another fifteen minutes."

"You mind if I call him?"

"Who?"

"The DA."

"You're getting smart."

"I've been listening to your stories for four years now, McCain. The chief didn't believe you, and neither do I."

"How about ten minutes?"

He glanced at Mary as if for guidance. To me he said: "How about five?"

"Five? What can I say in five minutes?"

"A lot, if you get right to it."

"How about seven?"

"How about six?"

Mary had been swallowing 7UP and almost spit it out laughing. "You two sound like seven-year-olds arguing about marbles."

"I'll take you back to his cell. And I'm starting the six-minute clock as soon as my key goes in the cell door."

He kept talking to me as we walked the corridors toward the back of the station where the cells were. I wasn't paying much attention. I was thinking of seeing the smile on Doran's face when I told him that I now had at least two more very possible suspects and would be telling the DA about one of them. Cliffie wouldn't release Doran on his own, but his DA cousin could force him to. Doran needed some good news. It didn't take long for most people to wither in a jail cell. Depression came fast; claustrophobia came even faster.

Like the rest of the station, the cell block was clean, well-lighted, well-windowed, even if the bars on them did spoil any thoughts of escape.

Doran was in a cell at the back. He sat bent over on his cot. I wondered if he was sick. If you haven't had jail experience, your body can retaliate.

He wasn't sick, though. He was scribbling on a yellow pad and when he turned his face up to mine, he didn't look wasted at all. He half shouted: "Hey, man! Great to see you!"

What the hell was he so happy about?

Tomlin's key made a scraping noise. "Six minutes, McCain. Starting now."

He locked me in and left. I sat on the cot across from Doran.

"You doing all right, Doran?"

"This is so cool," Doran said.

"What?"

"This — this is very, very cool, McCain."

"This is cool? Being in jail is cool? The last time I saw you, you were terrified."

"That's before I had my idea."

He was doing theater again. He was up on his feet and walking around as much as the cell allowed. He could have snapped. It's not unknown for people in jail to have breakdowns. Or even try suicide. "Listen, Doran, I think maybe I've got a shot at getting you out of here."

"Out of here! Are you crazy? You try and get me out of here, McCain, and I'll get another lawyer."

"Sit down."

"What?"

"I said sit down. I don't know what's wrong with you, but I think we better get the city psychologist to have a talk with you. Of *course* you want to get out of here. You're innocent — or at least I'm pretty sure you are."

He sat down and leaned forward and snapped, "What the hell kind of book will that make?"

"Book? What the hell are you talking about?"

"My life story. All the people I've claimed

to be. And how I wound up in jail falsely accused of a murder. And how a kind-of-down-on-his-luck lawyer saved my bacon."

No, he wasn't crazy; *I* was crazy. The words were supposed to be that he hated it in here and that he wanted to get out before he killed himself — but for some reason my brain wasn't tuned to the right radio station. I was hearing some insane bullshit about him writing a book and *wanting to stay in jail.*

"I've got to be in here for at least a week. So if you've figured out who killed the old man, you've got to keep it to yourself for at least five or six days. That'll give me my ending — you know — how if I hadn't been falsely accused, I wouldn't ever have looked back on my life and realized that I should never have let all those women support me, even though — you know — I pretty much paid them back when bedtime rolled around. It's the old Cecil B. DeMille stuff — fifty-five minutes of sin and five minutes of repenting at the end."

"I quit."

"What?"

"Unless you tell me right now that all this bullshit is a joke, I'm quitting."

"This is my chance, man. I used to sleep with this older woman in New York. She's a very important editor. I know she'll go for this."

I could hear Tomlin unlocking the door that opened on the jail.

"Look, you moron. They might convict you of this. They could get first degree. You could try diminished capacity because you were so drunk; but even if they knock it down to second, you're in prison for a long time."

"But you know I'm innocent. And you're a lawyer and a private detective and —"

"It's too much of a risk."

"But I'm *innocent!*"

"That doesn't mean I'll be able to turn up the killer, dipshit. Innocent people get convicted all the time."

I enjoyed seeing shock register on his pretty-boy face.

"Time's up, McCain," Tomlin said as he unlocked the cell.

I shook my head and started to walk out, but Doran grabbed me by the shoulder. "I still think the book's a great idea."

I was almost to the door when he shouted: "That editor'll love this!"

I wondered if I had enough in the bank to get him a year's worth of electroshock treatments.

■ ■ ■ ■

PART TWO

■ ■ ■ ■

13

One, two, three, four — I counted eight reporters including two with camera crews. The good Reverend Cartwright was getting the publicity he wanted. The crowd probably numbered seventy or eighty.

Nearest the growing heap of Beatles records, books, and other merchandise were Cartwright's people — stern mothers and fathers who pushed their small children forward to toss more sinful material on the pile. I noticed that there were few teenagers. They'd probably been harder to con into doing this, and the ones who did go along with it were the type who thought hall monitoring and snitching were more fun than abusing yourself.

Flanked around them were the sneerers. These were teenage boys who formed a Greek chorus of snickers, laughs, jeers, and mockery. Eventually one of them would fart and then they would fall about like drunks.

Then there were the rest of us, the curious. Cartwright was fun to watch and listen to. He was so full of shit, his blue eyes should have been brown. His problems with microphones alone were worth coming to see. For as long as he'd been at it — and for as many people as he had in his church, one or two of whom must have had some proficiency with the equipment — he was always at the mercy of every kind of mike on the market.

All this was taking place right after the Labor Day parade. I'd stood next to Sue and Kenny. The marching bands and small floats excited him as usual. He swayed to the snappy band music. I was waiting for him to start saluting. Sue and Kenny were going to Sue's folks' for the rest of the day, so I was at Cartwright's alone.

The side of the church where the Babylonian tower was growing by the minute had big pictures of the Fab Four taped to it. The witch hunters had scribbled all over their faces. There was also a huge poster of Jesus that looked more like a Marine recruiting poster than a celebration of an iconic religious figure. Cartwright was one of those ministers who constantly retold the Bible story of Jesus kicking the money lenders out of the temple. This was the story always used to justify religious violence aimed at those who didn't share your own beliefs. Jesus the gunfighter; Jesus the hit man. Having a great deal of respect for Jesus, man or son of God take your choice, I've always resented people who twist his life and words into a call for hatred and war.

As soon as I heard the high-decibel ear-melting sound of feedback, I knew that Cartwright was ready to go.

He'd fixed up a little dais for himself. He stood on it now, glaring at the stand-up microphone as if it might attack him. He flicked a finger at the head of the mike and then jerked back when it screeched at him. He wore his red robes today. They were vaguely papal. Before starting to speak, he raised a Bible-heavy right hand and showed it around to the crowd as if he was an auctioneer trying to get some bids on it.

And then he started. It was the same old bullshit. He was a lazy orator. He basically gave the same speech for all these publicity events. He just substituted whatever atrocity was at hand.

I formed the opening of his attack in my mind even before he spoke it: "Am I the only person in our community who is willing to fight the paganism that is perverting our children? No! Thank the good and

131

magnificent Lord I am not! Look at these concerned parents whose children are wise enough to recognize paganistic evil when they see it." He used the Bible to point at the mound of dirty low-down rock-and-roll stuff.

That was when thunder started rumbling across the sky that had turned gray-black halfway through the parade.

One of the sneerers shouted: "It's gonna rain, Reverend!"

"It will not start raining until God's will has been satisfied." And his flock started clapping so hard, you'd think he'd just given them a new Chevy.

And then he set off. The basic message was that there were kids in this very town who had thoughts about sex. Yes, *actual thoughts about actual sex,* those filthy little bastards.

These kids would have no interest in sex if they weren't encouraged by the "paganistic" smut that they could not escape.

Smut that was everywhere from magazines to movies to TV. The last one I didn't understand. I only knew of one smutty newscast. That being "Walter Cronkite and the Fucking News."

Then there was the music. He went through the list, starting with Mick Jagger and finishing up with "Communistic" folk singers.

But the Beatles were the worst of all because they made paganism seem "cute" and "friendly" even though this kind of charade was very typical of how the devil seduced otherwise innocent teenagers into breaking the laws of God.

Now, none of this would be remarkable if the tall, gaunt man with the bullet-shaped head and the red robes didn't break into holy song every few minutes — without warning and with no particular relevance to what he was shouting about. He went crazy. He raised his hands to the heavens and broke into a baffling bone-shattering dance, the Bible flying out of his hand, his mad eyes rolling back into his head and spittle like froth spewing from his lips. He'd obviously gone to the same divinity school as Little Richard, DDT.

This is what the press had come for. This was a maniac that *everybody* could laugh at, even other religious people. I always wondered if he knew he was a joke, or if he simply put up with the derision to get his message out because getting his message out emboldened his Visitors on their collection rounds. Now they'd be more like SS troops than ever before.

After about twenty minutes of this, he started to wear people out. It was hot, and ominous thunder rumbled constantly in the background. The youngest ones who'd been pushed forward had started to complain. They were bored and they wanted to go home.

Even the sneerers were quiet now. He'd won by the sheer brute force of boring people. He was just hitting the twenty-five-minute mark when the rain started pattering down. This wasn't to be a cleansing rain. This was a dusty summer rain with swollen drops that were hot on the skin.

"Now we will please the Lord! Now we will do our duty!"

For some reason these words seemed to rally the faithful out of their funk. They suddenly jerked their arms to the leaky heavens and shouted in unison, "Cleanse us, O Lord! Cleanse us!"

Cartwright broke into another quick song. In this one he claimed he'd rather be deaf, dumb, and blind than to be saturated with smut. Hey, Reverend, speak for yourself, all right?

And now came the ultimate moment.

He turned away for a few seconds, then reappeared holding a small red can with the word GASOLINE printed in yellow on the side of it. He was going to torch Ringo.

He raised the can above his head the way a priest raises the Eucharist right before Communion. "This is the Lord's judgment. I am doing this in the name of the Lord!"

Then he leaped from the dais. His landing worked against the drama. He nearly fell on his holy ass.

The gasoline in the can sloshing, he advanced on the tumbledown mass of rock-and-roll trash he planned to burn. The sneerers awakened, laughing and hooting as the rain began to intensify. Some of the flock turned around and shouted at them, but that only made the teenagers torment them more loudly.

Meanwhile, the good Reverend Cartwright was raising the gasoline can to the sky again. The eyes looked more crazed than ever.

One more time he raised the gasoline can. He really needed to get some new material for this part of his act. The can thing was almost as boring as his songs.

His benediction finished, he brought the can down and bent over to unscrew the cap.

By now the sneerers and three burly members of the church were standing inches apart insulting each other. Two of the print reporters were hovering over their notebooks so the paper wouldn't get drenched by the rain. One of them glanced up at me and grinned. This was good stuff for a story.

Standing behind him, out in the street with a few other onlookers, I saw the large, glowering shape of Roy Davenport. He saw me watching him. He rubbed his nose with his middle finger. A subtle man. We'd tangled verbally many times at city council meetings when Lou was using his surrogates to push through something that was good for him and bad for everybody else.

It was while I was staring at Davenport that it happened, so I can't say I was an eyewitness. But I sure heard the screams. I may even have heard the *whoosh* when Cartwright a) poured way too much gasoline on the goodies and b) stood way too close to the sudden explosion when it came.

I turned just in time to see the holy man's robes go up in flames while a wild, flailing pack of his believers flung themselves on him like jungle animals on a fresh carcass.

Even the sneerers shut up. Somebody shouted "Get an ambulance!"

The crowd broke into small groups, the way the crowd had at the anti-war rally the other night. I saw two or three women tip their foreheads to their Bibles and begin to pray.

The rain now came with enough force to *pop* when it hit. Umbrellas and newspapers and scarves went over heads at the same time that a cry went up from the people who'd rushed forward to help Cartwright.

I tried to push my way through a phalanx of believers, but they pushed and shoved back. They knew a pagan when they saw one. There was a sob, and I was pretty sure it came from Cartwright.

"God has prevailed!" somebody in the tight circle surrounding the religious man cried.

And damned if he wasn't right.

The circle opened so the rest of us could see Cartwright standing upright in his tattered and blackened robes. His smile was positively beatific. He waved to us with papal majesty. Into the crowd, into the day, he shouted: "God loves me! The only thing that got burned were my robes!"

I have to admit the son of a bitch looked pretty good to me right then. Sure he was a con artist and a showboat, but he'd been around us so long now that he was one of us. And I was happy to see he was all right, if only because he was a lot funnier than most of the comedy shows on the tube.

Voices shouted prayers of gratitude to the surly skies, and flock members rushed forward to touch him.

My elation lasted only about forty-two seconds before I was back to seeing him for the snake he was. Besides, I wanted to talk to Roy Davenport.

I didn't see him. I was already wet, so I decided I might as well get soaked. I rushed among the parked cars in the lot, gaping into windshields. I had no idea what kind of automobile he was driving. Then I saw him across the street and down the block about a quarter of the way. He was walking toward a big-ass black Pontiac. The rain was at the slashing stage now, blinding me as I ran down the middle of the street. Everywhere people were running to get away from the suddenly furious deluge, ducking into shop fronts and under awnings. But not Davenport. Head down, he walked slowly toward the sleek black Pontiac Bonneville. Even parked, the new car seemed to throb with power.

I called his name a few times, but he didn't turn around to see who was chasing him. I caught up with him, splashing across the pavement. I grabbed his arm. He jerked away and gave me a shove that pushed me back two feet.

"I need to talk to you," I said above the pounding rain.

My shoes were filling with water. So were my eyes and ears. My clothes were heavy with water. "When was the last time you talked to Lou Bennett?" I shouted at his back as he bent over to unlock his car.

He didn't answer me. He just started to open the door. I probably wouldn't have done it if I'd had to think it through. I rushed at him, slamming the door shut before he could stop me.

He moved so fast I wasn't sure what he was doing, until an enormous hand clutched my throat, started choking me. I could hear people shouting as they realized what was going on. I managed to hit him hard on the side of his eye. His hands loosened enough for me to pull out of his grasp. Then he shoved me again. The wet surface of the street worked like ice. I skidded backward several feet, doing a silent comedy routine of wheeling arms and stumbling feet as I tried to stay upright. But it didn't work. I landed on my butt, landed hard enough that I was stunned when my body slammed the concrete. I just sat there then getting wetter and wetter, watching him get into his Bonneville. My throat was raw from where he'd choked me.

I could have stayed there awhile, I suppose, but the cars honking for me to get out of the way made me change my mind. Getting soaked and choked was enough for right now. I wasn't quite ready for getting run over.

I drank a beer and read about a third of Graham Greene's *It's a Battlefield* while I soaked in a tub of water so hot, they probably could have served me as an entrée to cannibals. My cat Tasha kept me company by dozing on top of the clothes hamper. I had a Gene Pitney album blasting in the living area.

The hot water had taken care of my scratchy throat. By the time I'd climbed the rear steps to my apartment, I was sneezing. The sneezing was gone now, too.

I finished by taking a brief cold shower before grabbing my terrycloth robe and going into the kitchen area and shoving a TV dinner into the oven. Sometimes they tasted better with the aluminum foil on. I tried not to remember Jane saying that after we were married, TV dinners would be banned forever from that misty sentimental mythic home we'd be building.

I ate as always in front of the TV set. There had been small anti-war protests across the country, the only one of note being in Berkeley. The local channels would be running the stories about Lou Bennett's murder and the anti-war meeting that had preceded it.

I was shoving myself into T-shirt and jeans when the phone rang. These days, a call had a paralyzing effect on me. Maybe my heart even stopped for a single second. Would it be Jane? And if it was Jane, what would she say? And if it was Jane, what would *I* say?

A woman crying: "Have you talked to him?" I wasn't quite sure who it was until she said: "This book idea is insane."

When I realized who it was, I almost smiled. Was she finally seeing him as I saw him? "I'm not his lawyer any more, Molly."

"They'll convict him. He doesn't seem to understand that." Then: "I just worked up enough courage to call you now."

"Didn't he tell you that I'd talked to him?"

"He said he'd fired you."

"Of course he said he'd fired me. It'll make a better story for the book. I quit, is what happened. He's going to get in so deep, he'll never get out. He lives in a fantasy world, Molly."

"But I love him so much. I don't care how much he lies or cheats or steals."

"He steals?"

"Just cars. And not all that often."

"Ah."

"You're so judgmental, McCain."

"Yes, I even thought that Hitler wasn't all that nice a guy."

"You and your sarcasm. Now you have to help him. You just *have* to."

At least she'd quit crying. I decided to try and make her feel better. "I'm still working on the case. I think he's innocent. But I'm not doing this for him, Molly. He's a jerk."

"He's not a jerk. He's artistic, and most people don't know how to handle artistic people."

Not much I could say to that. If bunco artist was a synonym for artistic, fine, he was artistic.

"Will you tell me the minute you find something, so I know he'll be all right?"

"Sure, Molly. But there aren't any guarantees."

"But you and the judge always prove that Cliffie's wrong."

"There's always a first time, Molly."

"But you know he's *innocent.*"

"I'll do what I can, Molly. The best thing you can do is visit him as often as Cliffie will let you and bring him cigarettes and any food you can."

"He wants to be a painter and actor and symphony composer, McCain. And I know if I just support him for a few years, he'll be able to be all those things. That way he won't have to, you know, steal stuff any more. We've already talked about it."

Jamie had a bullshit artist who'd started a surfing band in Iowa, and now Molly had a bullshit artist who was going to rival Leonard Bernstein while also giving Brando and Gauguin a run for their money.

"I'll get back to you, Molly."

"I really appreciate this, McCain. I'm sure he'll give you one of his paintings and it'll be worth millions some day."

"Uh-huh."

"I can tell you're sneering. But I'm serious. People will be falling all over themselves to buy his paintings."

"That's because they'll be drunk. Blind drunk."

"You're so smug, McCain. That was probably one of the reasons I didn't fall in love with you."

"Because I'm smug?"

"Yes."

"Good. I was afraid it was because I didn't know Joan Baez."

"God, you're so childish. You don't recognize a great artist even when you see one."

"Molly —" But what was the use? I was just bitter because I looked on guys like Elmer Fudd and Turk as masterminds of a sort. Not only did they get women to give them sex and shelter; they got them to support them in their fantasy lives.

"Molly, I'm sorry about being such a jerk. You believe in him, and that's good enough for me."

"Are you setting me up for a joke?"

"Nope. I like you. We're friends. So I want to help you."

"Jeez, that's really nice of you, thanks. And I shouldn't have said that about you being smug. I mean for the reason I didn't fall in love with you."

"That's all right."

"I mean, technically I didn't fall in love with you for other reasons. But there's no point going into them now, is there? We're friends and that's all that matters. Thanks again, McCain."

I had another Hamm's and sat with my bare feet on the coffee table while cats Tasha and Crystal slept on my outstretched legs. I tried not to think about the "other reasons" Molly hadn't fallen in love with me. But of course I did. Not fall in love with me? How was that possible?

Around seven thirty, the phone rang again. I reached behind the couch to the small table where I'd dragged it.

"I had dinner out tonight, Sam, or I

would've told you earlier."

It was my landlady, Mrs. Goldman, the one who looks like Lauren Bacall will at sixty. If Bacall is lucky.

"You got six or seven calls this afternoon. I was hanging laundry in the back yard. Somebody really wanted to get hold of you."

Not Molly: she said she'd just worked up the courage to call earlier. I thought of my father. Six or seven calls. Had my mother been trying to find me?

"Well, whoever it was hasn't called back. But I appreciate you telling me."

"I'm sorry I had to be in Iowa City last night, Sam. Otherwise I would've been with you at that rally."

"How'd it go for your night out?"

"I met a man at the synagogue. A very nice man." The warmth of her voice told me that she was smiling. She was a sixtyish widow, bright, beautiful, and great company. Many eligible widowers had courted her, but as yet none had won her. She was worth the effort.

"Remember, I get to sing at your wedding."

She laughed. "I've heard you sing. How much would you need to *not* sing at my wedding?"

As soon as we finished, I dialed home. I

145

heard a TV Western going strong in the background. My mother, after I asked if she'd tried to get in touch with me, said, "No, everything's fine, honey. There are three Westerns on tonight and your dad's enjoying every one of them."

By eight thirty, I was in bed with the cats sleeping all around me. I dreamed of sleeping with Wendy Bennett. I'm not sure what the cats dreamed about.

14

Twelve hours later, following another shower and wearing a fresh short-sleeved white shirt and blue trousers, I pushed into the chambers of Her Most Sacred Excellency Esme Anne Whitney and stared in disbelief as she raised a glass of whiskey to her lips. All her struggles with sobriety, lost.

My impulse was to race across the long office, dive at her desk, and wrench the drink from her slender hand.

She had the newspaper spread out and was so taken with whatever she was reading, she apparently didn't hear me come in.

"Morning, Judge."

Her head came up slowly. She offered me her usual reluctant smile — be nice to the slaves, but not *too* nice — and then said, "What the hell are you gaping at, McCain?"

"Oh, nothing, I guess."

"You're giving me the creeps."

"I'm giving *you* the creeps?"

"Will you please tell me what the hell you're staring at?"

"What the hell am I staring at? Your drink. Your — whiskey."

"Whiskey?" She raised her glass as if toasting me and then began laughing in a way that was almost bawdy and very much out of character for the pride of rich snobs everywhere. "My God, McCain. Are you really that stupid? This is ginger ale. I'm tired of Coke."

I guess my skepticism was obvious.

"Here, you idiot. Come over here and smell it."

"It's really ginger ale?"

"No, McCain, it's really bourbon and I'm about to jump up on my desk and start dancing. Would you be happy if I did that?"

"It just looked —"

"Oh, God, how did you get through law school?"

"I mowed the professor's lawn every other Saturday."

"I don't doubt that. Now get over here and tell me more about this fool Cliffie's got in jail."

I had called her about seven thirty to make sure she'd be in. I had given her a few sketchy details about Doran. I told her I'd tell her the rest when we met in her chambers.

"He really thinks he won't be prosecuted and convicted?" she asked as I sat down.

The linen suit today was mauve with a silk bone-colored blouse. She was a damned good-looking woman, as she well knew. She was even better-looking now that she'd given up alcohol.

"His girlfriend thinks I'll solve the case and by then he'll have enough material for his book."

"I want to solve the case — God, imagine if Cliffie actually beats us, what that would do to my family honor, a Whitney being bested by a Sykes — but there's always a first time."

"That's what I told her."

"He hasn't confessed, I hope?"

"No. But he told them he doesn't remember everything. And there's a witness who puts him out in front of the mansion."

"You Reds are certainly dopes."

"I'm not a Red and neither is he. I'm a Democrat and he's a con artist who's using the anti-war movement to get girls and mooch room and board."

"Admirable. Trotsky would have loved him." She took a long drink and then smiled coldly at me. "Bourbon is so refreshing at eight thirty in the morning."

"Very funny."

She leaned back. The posture and the cold gray eyes told me she was all judge now. "Poor Lou."

"You feel sorry for him, but not for all the kids he wanted to send to Vietnam. He was a warmonger."

"I'm not going to let you get away with that, McCain. Whatever else he might or might not have been, Lou Bennett was a patriot. We don't have any choice. We have to fight this war. And you and your beatnik friends aren't going to stop us with your childish demonstrations."

I would have clicked my heels, but I wasn't wearing the right kind of shoes.

There are two kinds of relationships that get the most attention in Black River Falls. Divorces and the dissolution of business partnerships. The first is always juicier, because most of the time there is an extra lover involved. You get to scorn somebody and feel morally superior. That's hard to beat.

Business partner break-ups rarely involve sex, but they do sometimes involve extralegal activities such as fraud and embezzlement. Even without breasts and trysts being mentioned, such nefarious business practices can get pretty interesting. Three years ago, two men who owned the same bar got into a fight after hours, and one killed the other with a tire iron. That's not as good as the high-school teacher who impregnated one of his students her senior year, but it'll do on a slow night.

Roy Davenport had been partners with Lou Bennett in three businesses, all related to agriculture. A farm implement store, a dairy, and a trucking company that delivered cattle to slaughterhouses. Davenport and Bennett were distant relatives — I got all this information by calling Kenny as soon as I left the judge's office — and the proper part of the business community was not happy that Bennett would choose to work with a man who had a criminal record. He'd served four years at the Fort Madison penitentiary for embezzling from the used-car lot where he'd worked over in Moline. Bennett defended his man by saying that he deserved a second chance, an odd comment coming from Bennett, given his belief that every citizen above age twelve should be tried as an adult.

I wanted to talk to Davenport about his relationship with Bennett. All I knew so far was that a woman named Sally Crane had come between them.

I thought of this as I pulled my ragtop up the slanting gravel drive that led to a green ranch-style house that spread all the way across the long hilltop. A man in jean cut-offs and a Cubs T-shirt was spraying water from a hose, obviously trying to raise the dead brown grass that covered the hill. The sun had scorched everything.

He had a cigar in his mouth, and when he glanced up from his watering, his eyes fixed on me with anger and malice. Roy Davenport was the scourge of Rotary and the scourge of city council meetings. He brooked no fools. The problem was that he considered everybody but himself to be a fool.

I parked and got out of the car. I started walking toward him. He aimed the hose at me. We played a little game. I'd jump aside just as he'd try to spray me. He could have splashed me any time he wanted to, but I guess this was more fun for him. He got the lower part of my trousers once. He laughed behind his cigar. Finally he threw the hose aside and said, "Hold it right there, McCain. What the hell're you doing here?"

We were still ten yards apart. His legs were spread, and he was punching a fist into the palm of the opposite hand as if he was ready for a brawl.

"I want to talk to you about Lou Bennett."

"Then you wasted your trip. I've got nothing to say."

"Did you kill him?"

He had a good big theatrical laugh for me. "Sure. You got a confession I can sign?"

"From what I hear, you had a good reason. I think her name was Sally Crane."

"You've been hanging around that little newspaper girl, Molly or whatever her name is. She wouldn't let go of it either, when Lou and I parted company. Good thing she's got some nice tits, or I would've been a whole lot rougher with her."

"Hate to disappoint you. She wasn't the one who told me."

The door from the breezeway opened, and a vision in a white bikini appeared. She was ridiculously blonde and ridiculously voluptuous. And tanned. She did the kind of runway walk a girl can learn only from a small-town modeling school, way too stiff and way too self-conscious. She came bearing a large glass jar of what appeared to be pickles.

Unlike the master of the place, she had a smile for me. She held the jar up with both hands and said, "I can't get the lid off. I don't know why they put these on so tight."

I had to retrieve my eyes from somewhere deep inside her bikini top. She probably hadn't read much Chaucer, but what the hell.

She carried the jar over to Davenport. He was swelling himself up to play the hero here. He put out a big paw and then closed it around the jar as she handed it to him.

He had a he-man chuckle for her. "Good thing I'm around, or you'd be in a hell of a fix."

"I sure would be, Roy." She was a supplicant now, worshipping this godlike being with a look of wonder in her empty green eyes.

Elmer Fudd, Turk, Roy Davenport — did they know the real true secret of getting and holding women?

I have to say I enjoyed it. The big man set upon the jar with scorn and purpose in his eyes. He even glanced at me as if to say *Watch, this is how one tough sumbitch takes care of a jar lid.*

The first time he tried to open it, nothing happened. He lifted it up and glared at it as if it wasn't what it appeared to be. Somebody had obviously given him a ringer. This lid must've been welded on. This must've been one of those gags they pulled on unsuspecting strangers on *Candid Camera.*

He tried again, of course. No luck this time either. The third time he went at it, his face got red and his eyes began to bulge.

"Are you all right, Roy?" the girl said.

"Shut up, Pauline."

The fourth time he vised the jar between his knees. I could have pointed out that this would make getting any kind of serious grip on the lid just about impossible, but that would've spoiled my fun. I just watched.

He had no luck with the knee approach, nor with the next one, the under-the-arm routine. "What the hell are you lookin' at, McCain? Get your ass off my property."

"You're not going to fight again, are you, Roy?" She sounded nervous, maybe even scared.

"How about letting *me* try it?" I said.

The distant sounds of trucks on the highway, of birds and dogs and a hot breeze pushing the abundant leaves of the oaks and hardwoods of the windbreak.

"I guess you didn't hear me, McCain. You get the hell off my land."

I didn't blame him, really. Most men, me included, want to look competent and cool and strong. A person of the female extraction hands you a jar with a tight lid and you want to John Wayne it. You want to hear that *pop* when the jar opens and you want to

155

feel the moist lips on your cheek when she retrieves the jar from your outsize manly hands and gives you a kiss of eternal feminine gratitude.

"Maybe he can help us, Roy —"

"You shut the hell up and get back in the house and take this damned jar with you. You hear me?"

"But you always want pickles on your burgers."

"Well, maybe this time I don't."

There was real pain in her dark eyes. She'd failed her master. She took the jar from him and lowered her head in shame.

When she turned to walk back to the house, she cut a wide path. I don't think she intended to. I think she was feeling so rejected she wasn't paying any attention to where she was walking. But she came so close to me that I didn't have any trouble lifting the jar from her hands.

"Hey —" she started to object.

"You son of a bitch. You give her that jar back."

My dad has a trick. It doesn't always work. And it only works after you've tried to open the jar a few times by conventional means.

I raised my knee. I banged the jar once against my kneecap, then kept turning it so that I hit it on different sides, just the way my old man does. I did this very quickly. And just as quickly, I clamped the jar into one hand and started wrestling with the lid. It popped open.

She started to smile but realized what that would get her. It would get her Roy. She swiped the jar from me and said, "You shouldn't ought to have done that." Then she stomped away. She wanted to make sure that Roy understood how much she hated me.

Roy picked the hose up again. He held his thumb over the tip so it wouldn't spray.

"She's right, asshole. You shouldn't ought to have done that."

"Bad for your image, huh?"

"Nah, bad for your health."

"I think I heard that one on *Dragnet* last night."

"Lou and me had our problems. I hated him, but I didn't hate him enough to kill him. And that's all you need to know. And if you think I'm shittin' you about it bein' bad for your health, just keep pushing and you'll find out."

I smiled at him. I couldn't beat him in a fight, but I sure could have the pleasure of irritating the hell out of him. "First you choke me and now I bet you're going to spray me when I walk back to my car. I

don't think a real tough guy would do that
— it's kind of a sissy thing if you ask me —
but it's your call. Roy. You want to be a sissy
and spray me, it's up to you."

And with that I started the trip back to
my ragtop, congratulating myself on my use
of reverse psychology. By telling him it was
a sissy thing to do, I'd ensured he wouldn't
spray me. Who wants to get wet?

When I was about ten feet from the ragtop, he started spraying the hell out of me.

15

After getting into dry clothes, I walked over to the library.

Trixie Easley was explaining the Dewy Decimal System to an impatient-looking high-school girl wearing a Stones T-shirt. I was hoping Trixie would explain it to me when she finished with the girl. I waved to her and walked to the back of the library where the newspaper files are kept in outsize bound books.

Lynn Shanlon's words about the fire that had taken her sister's life had stayed with me, at least enough to make me want to read up on it.

I had no trouble finding the story. Coverage spread over four days, ending with a photo of the funeral service. Each piece included a reference to smoking in bed. There was no mention of the fact that she rarely smoked.

There was a sidebar with a photo of the

man who had the final say on the origins of the blaze, Fire Chief Ralph DePaul. Sight of him made my stomach clench and my jaw tighten. I'd had many run-ins with this self-appointed protector of All That Was Right and Good in our community. He was always hinting that there were Communists teaching our children and pornography being sold under the counter in two different stores. A few times, he came close to naming Kenny as a Commie pornographer, but backed off. He was smart enough to know that Kenny would sue him.

His conclusion was that the fire had been accidental due to smoking. He then started into his stump speech about American values. He made it sound as if we were the only country that tried to do anything about fires. Apparently, foreigners just let their homes burn down without trying to stop the flames in any way. DePaul was always announcing that he was planning to announce that he was running for mayor, but somehow he never got around to it.

There was very little about Karen Marie Shanlon. She lived and died without making much of an impression on the town; that was the sense of the biographical material. Born, graduated high school, worked as a secretary, never married, died. The cold statistics that define most of us. No mention of her gracious beauty, the limp that had always kept her an outsider, the love her sister felt for her.

I closed the big book and sat there for a time. I should have been thinking about poor Karen. Instead, I was thinking about how much I despised Fire Chief DePaul.

The temperature was July, but the slant and quality of sunlight was autumn, the golden color thinner and not as burnished. I used to hike in the woods, and I became aware of how different the sunlight is season to season. I once tried explaining this on a first date. Can you guess why there wasn't a second date?

I took note of this as I stood on the courthouse steps watching the black Lincoln four-door sedan pull into the parking lot on the east side of the building. This was the official Lou Bennett mobile. There was a new one every year. The driver was William Hughes. I couldn't remember ever seeing Bennett drive it.

Hughes wore a tan summer suit and a crisp Panama hat. He had always been smooth and quick in indulging his employer, but now his age seemed to have slowed him. Or maybe it was just the heat. He didn't see me until he was halfway up the broad staircase. He peered at me from under the brim of his Panama. A frown formed on his lips, and his eyes showed a sudden irritation. I had the sense that of all the people in town, I was the one he least wanted to see.

I walked three steps down to meet him. "I'd really like to talk to you, William."

He had a manila folder in one large hand. He held it up as if he was going to demonstrate it, like a product on TV. "I have business with the county clerk inside here, McCain, and that's the only business I intend to do today. I'm supposed to file some papers since Mr. Bennett was killed. Linda said she needs me back home as soon as possible. She's not holding together real well."

"Linda and David are two of the people I want to talk to you about."

"I don't have to talk to you and I don't intend to."

I followed his gaze. He was trying to figure out what it would take to get around me and hurry up the stairs. But his dark face was sheened with sweat and the way he'd come up the steps told me he wasn't capable of hurrying. He was no longer a young man.

"You won't make it, William. I'll follow

162

you inside and then I'll wait outside the county clerk's office and I'll walk you to your car and be a real pain in the ass. That doesn't sound like much fun, does it?"

This time he glanced all the way up the stairs to the three glass doors leading into the shadowy interior that was cooled by air conditioning. He sighed. "Let's get some iced tea at that stand in there."

The stand inside served hamburgers and potato salad and drinks. I had coffee and he had iced tea. There were four small tables where visitors and courthouse employees could sit and talk. People of every kind passed our table — fancy lawyers reassuring clients that everything would be fine, working-class men obtaining different kinds of permits, frightened mothers guiding their sullen boys into juvenile court — the foot-steps of all of them melding and echoing off the high marble walls of the courthouse that dated back to FDR's Depression money.

Hughes took off his Panama, wiped his forehead with a folded brown handkerchief. "So what is it you want, McCain?"

"I want to know who killed your boss."

"According to Chief Sykes, we already know."

"Chief Sykes is usually wrong."

"Not in this case. This Doran was out at

the house at three A.M. We don't usually get visitors that late."

"And that's about all Sykes has got as evidence."

"If you say so."

I offered him a smoke. He shook his head.

"How did Linda and David Raines get along with Bennett?"

"I never talk about the family. Never."

"If I was a cynic, that would make me think you're hiding something."

"I can't help what you think, McCain."

He paused to wave at somebody who passed by. He was good at what he did. He had the voice and manner of a good physician. He put you at ease. He reassured. But he was lying. I was sure of it.

"So you pretty much think Doran killed Bennett?"

"Who else would have, Mr. McCain? It's obvious, isn't it?"

"Not to me."

"Of course not. You're his lawyer. You have to say that."

"Technically, I'm not his lawyer. I've resigned."

For the first time the wise brown eyes studied me. I'd surprised him, and he didn't care for surprises. He seemed to be one of those men whose life was laid out like a

164

map. He knew the land and he knew what to expect. "Now, that I haven't heard. Do you mind if I ask why?"

I smiled. "I never talk about my cases. Never. Sound familiar?"

He waved to somebody, then leaned toward me. "You're making this a lot more complicated than it needs to be, McCain. We know who killed Mr. Bennett. There's no need to go into Mr. Bennett's life looking for trash. He lived as an honorable man. Let him die that way, too."

"What're you afraid of?"

He eased himself out of his chair. He picked his hat up, took one more swipe across his face with his handkerchief, and said, "What am I afraid of? I'm afraid that if I don't get up to the second floor right now, I'll be late for my appointment. That's what I'm afraid of, McCain."

"You could've been killed," Jamie was saying to the man in the chair. From behind, I didn't recognize him at first. It was the blond hair. Turk's hair had been dark. I hadn't realized that he'd bleached it.

He sat in one of the two client chairs in front of my desk. There was a mean-looking black-red circle about the size of a dime on the back of his head. Bright blood had coursed down from there, leaking into the edge of his white T-shirt.

I walked around for a look at him, and that was when I saw the mess on the floor in front of the filing cabinets. Somebody had been in a hurry. Piles of manila folders lay on the floor.

"Turk could've been killed, Mr. C."

"What happened?" I asked Turk, looking at the SURF BUMS logo on his T-shirt. I was pretty sure he'd drawn it on. It seemed to be a surfboard with a beard.

He was too much of a punk to answer me without trying to sound tough. "I ever catch that guy, he'll wish he'd never been born."

"Just tell me what happened, Turk."

He winced as Jamie dabbed at his wound with a wet cloth I suspected was her handkerchief.

Turk had the looks and sneer of most teen idols. What he didn't have was the talent. So he tried to compensate for it by mixing James Dean and Marlon Brando. We weren't having a conversation. We were in Acting Class 101.

"Jamie wasn't here when I got here —"

"I was out getting supplies like you told me to, Mr. C —"

"So I decided to wait outside and have a smoke. That way I could hear the car radio

166

if I turned it up. Brian has a new song out."

"He means Brian Wilson, Mr. C. You know, the Beach Boys?"

"Ah."

"But it's a funny thing, man. There I am sitting on the steps out there just groovin' with the new Animals song — they'd be a lot bigger if Eric Burdon wasn't so ugly — and then I hear it." He meant to touch his ear to illustrate his point, but when he got his hand about halfway to his head he winced and said, "Shit, man." He'd really been hit. "I got what you call 20/20 hearing, you know?"

"Sure, 20/20 hearing. Got it. So what did you hear?"

"Whaddya think I heard? I heard somebody in here. You know, your office. And then I put it together."

"Put what together?"

"The scene, man. The scene and what was happening. He'd been tossing your office before I got there, but when he heard me coming he disappeared. He hid, is what I mean. So I go in and look for Jamie, and when she's not there I leave. And then guess what he does?"

"He goes back to my office and starts going through the file cabinets again."

"See, Turk," Jamie said, "I told you Mr. C

wasn't stupid."

"So you come back into my office —"

"Correction. I *sneak* back into your office."

"Ah, the old sneakeroosky. Then what?"

"He faked me out."

"I'm not following you."

"He hid again. Before I got into the office. He must've been hiding in the hall."

"He must have heard you coming."

"Yeah, it was probably when I tripped on the steps outside. I probably cussed or something."

"You tripped?"

The insolent smile. "Me and Mary Jane got together a little while ago."

"Mary Jane is marijuana, Mr. C."

"So you're smoking dope and trying to sneak in. But you're stoned and you trip. You gave him plenty of warning."

"That's your version, man. My version is I scared him off. He doesn't want to tangle with me. He's had a chance to see me, so he knows he's dead if I ever get my hands on him. So he splits." Not only was Turk's bravado irritating, it was foolish. His arms had no definition, he had tiny wrists, and he was getting a small potbelly from all the beer Jamie's money was buying. "You dig?"

"He doesn't split, he hides. And he lets

168

you go into my office again and then he slugs you across the back of the head, and while you're unconscious he goes back to trashing my office."

"You bet your ass he hits me from the back. He ever tried it from the front, I'd rip him apart."

"Turk is very strong, Mr. C."

"Uh-huh." I pointed at his eyes. "Open them as wide as you can."

"No way, man. You're not no doctor."

"Very perceptive of you to recognize that, Turk. Must be your 20/20 hearing." To Jamie I said: "Doc Mayburn is just down the street. Take Turk down there and have him checked. He'll probably need a few stitches in that wound anyway."

"Stitches? No way, man. I had to have eight of them one time when I was six. I fell out of a tree and landed headfirst."

It would be too easy to point out that landing on his head might explain a lot of things about the latter-day Turk, but I liked Jamie too much to say it. Besides, I wanted to try and figure out what the asshole burglar had been looking for.

"Go on now. Tell Doc Mayburn to put it on my account."

"You think he has a concussion, Mr. C?"

"Well, he's got something, that's for sure."

169

"Here, honey, let me help you up."

"I ain't no invalid."

Jamie looked as if her new puppy had just been run over by the train.

Turk got up. He jerked in pain and grabbed his head. At least I was getting a little pleasure out of this. "We've got band practice tonight."

"Oh, no, Turk. You're in no condition to practice."

"Have to. Next week we send our tape to Dick Clark."

She beamed at me. "Isn't that cool, Mr. C? He'll be on *Bandstand* in no time."

"If the conditions are right. Don't forget that. I don't want no crummy background the way the rest of those bands get. I want somethin' really sharp."

"He's got a good business head, too, Mr. C."

"I can see that. Dick Clark doesn't know what he's in for."

By then, thankfully, they were in the hall and edging toward the door.

"No stitches, remember."

After they were gone, I started picking up file folders and putting them back in their proper places. I gave each one a minute or so of consideration. I was trying to figure out if one of them was the reason the thief had been in here. But most of them were old and pedestrian. Mortgages, divorces, wills — nothing that would be worth stealing.

When I was finishing up, I realized that this was a ruse, dumping everything out this way. He was searching for something else, and the piles of folders were nothing more than a distraction for my sake. Like many attorneys, I was file-rich and money-poor. But I'd never worked on a case that would prompt somebody to toss my office. Until now, the murder of Lou Bennett and the aftermath.

Since there was only one possible explanation, I went to my desk and opened the manila folder on it. I'd made copies of the material about Karen Shanlon's death in the fire. There were six sheets in all. I had put them in order of the date on which the newspaper story had been published. When I went through them now, they were out of sequence.

I went back and finished the filing. I walked down the hall and got a Pepsi from the machine, and then came back to try and think this through. The thief obviously thought I had something he didn't want me to have. And it had to do with the Karen Shanlon fire.

A picture of DePaul stared up at me from the folder. He'd been the chief at the time of the fire; he'd been the authority who'd called it accidental. I found myself thinking the unthinkable and enjoying the hell out of it. What if DePaul, the great patriot and overseer of public virtue, had taken a bribe? It wasn't exactly unheard of. Big town or small, a certain number of public officials were always on the take.

Since DePaul was the man who'd written the report on the fire that killed Karen Shanlon, he was the man I needed to start with.

I was halfway out of my chair when the phone rang. I answered and heard: "Somebody really hurt him, Sam. *Really hurt him!*"

Sue was usually an unflappable woman. Her presence allowed Kenny to be as flappable as he wanted to be and still function. But right now Sue was angry and scared and confused.

I pretty much knew what she was going to say but I let her say it anyway.

"I came home and I found Kenny on the ground in front of the trailer. He was facedown. I thought he was dead. There was so much blood on the back of his head."

"Where are you now?"

"Here. Home. But I'm headed to the

172

hospital emergency room. Could you meet us there?"

"Absolutely. I'll leave now."

"He still hasn't told me what you two are working on — he never tells me until afterward — but I want your promise that you'll stop."

What else could I say? "I'll stop, Sue. I promise. Now I'll see you at the hospital."

16

The medicinal scents of the emergency room brought back memories of the three times I'd spent in the hospital. I'd had my tonsils out, I'd broken my leg falling off the top of the garage, and I ran a fever the doc thought might affect my brain and heart. All this before I was nine years old. There were bonuses for being in the hospital. I got all the comic books I wanted, and I didn't have to pay for them with my own allowance. I remember especially a certain issue of Hawkman teaming up with Batman. I also got chocolate malts and a radio that seemed to play only the shows I wanted to hear. Sometimes being in the hospital is within pissing distance of being outright fun.

I had time for a cigarette and a cup of hospital coffee before Sue appeared with her arm around Kenny's waist. They wore contrasting expressions. Sue appeared to be ready for his funeral; Kenny smiled at me.

He had blood all over his short-sleeved blue shirt.

She got him into the seat next to me and said, "You make sure he doesn't move, Sam. He's in pretty bad shape." Then she was off to fill out forms so that Kenny could see a doc.

"The bastard was good, McCain. He must have come up from the creek behind my trailer and waited me out. I came out of the trailer to take a break — you know how I walk around sometimes because I get stiff sitting at the typewriter? — and he got me as soon as I got on the ground. Just came right up behind me and wham! I was out."

"You didn't get a look at him?"

"Nothing." For the first time his face crosshatched with pain. "I may have a little concussion. But man, Sue has gone batshit."

"She loves you."

"Yeah, but why?"

"Lots of people are asking the very same question."

"What the hell was he looking for at *my* place?"

"I may be wrong, but I think this has something to do with the fire that killed Karen Shanlon. You've been asking around about Lou Bennett and so have I. And I've been to the library reading up on the fire.

Somebody thinks we either know something or are about to find something out. He can't be sure which it is, so he has to make sure we don't already have something. He trashed my office, too. Knocked out Turk."

"Well, then he can't be *all* bad." But his face twisted up when he tried to laugh. Up close he looked pale and shaken. The blood on his shirt was lurid, like blood in a crime-scene photo.

"I promised Sue we'd pull back on this. Just forget about it."

"Are you crazy? Now I really want to go after him."

"Sorry. I promised Sue. I can break my word to her, but you can't break yours."

"I didn't give her my word. *You* gave her my word. So that doesn't count."

"You want to tell her that? You remember what happened the last time you broke your word to her?"

"Yeah. Spam the whole week."

"Right. And you're lucky she didn't leave the goop on when she served it to you."

"She had steak every night and I had Spam. She's a lot meaner than she looks."

Sue came back with a smiling nurse pushing a wheelchair. "Right in here, Mr. Thibodeau."

"I can walk."

"I'm sure you can. But these are hospital rules." The nurse was middle-aged and had learned how to be sweet while she was slapping you around with rules.

When he was safely seated, Sue bent over and kissed him on top of his head. Then she looked at me: "You gave your word, Sam."

"I did."

"And I expect you to keep it. *Both* of you."

"Maybe we could talk about that a little, honey."

"Are you ready, Mr. Thibodeau? We're going right down the hall and get you all fixed up. You may come with us if you like, Mrs. Thibodeau."

Sue had elevated herself to wife status. I glanced at her and smiled. She scowled. Kenny should never have said that "maybe we could talk about that a little, honey." The "honey" hadn't helped at all. It was clear there'd be no talking about it. Not with Sue. Not ever.

I saw a doctor and another nurse go into the room where Kenny had been wheeled. Sue appeared about fifteen minutes later. The hospital coffee was withering my vital organs.

She came over and sat down next to me. "I feel stupid, Sam. I really overreacted."

"You were worried."

"I still should have been able to control myself." She reached over and put her hand on mine. "I want to be a good mother."

"I'm sure you will be. You got upset. So what? We all get upset. We just get scared."

"Kenny doesn't know this yet, Sam. I'm pregnant. Six months from now, I'll be a mother and Kenny will be a father."

So there you had it. The best news that Kenny would receive in his life. Better even than selling "Sex Sirens of the Watery Deep" to *Real Balls Adventure.*

"Wow."

"I guess when I saw him there on the ground, all I could think of was that our baby wouldn't have a father. And I'd be devastated if anything happened to him. He's my life. You know how I always say that living with him is good practice for raising a kid? It's true. And that's what I love about him. He's so vulnerable. He doesn't worry about all the crap most men do." Then: "A baby. Pretty good news, right, Sam?" She looked like a kid herself just then. A very happy kid.

"The best news of all."

"Well, I'd better get back in there. No concussion and just four stitches." She took her hand from mine. "So now it's more important than ever that you two stay out of this thing — whatever it is."

I almost told her. I almost said, Here's the deal, Sue. I'm going to tell Kenny that I'm honoring my promise, that I'm giving this thing up completely. But I'll be working on it on the sly. He won't know, so he won't be tempted to help me. Is that a fair deal, Sue?

But I didn't. This was her moment. Her news, her baby, her joy. And I was going to tell her that I was going to break my word?

She kissed me on the cheek and then walked back to the room where Kenny was being patched up. I wondered where and when she'd tell him. I could feel myself grinning. In six months, the world would have one more soft-core porn writer.

Fire Chief DePaul lived in a new housing development on the east edge of town. The houses were painted in pastels. His was eggshell white. The lots here were about twice the size of the town's other developments and the construction appeared to be considerably better. A new Ford sedan and a new Chrysler sat in the drive. As I walked up to the front door, I noticed that many of the drives had new cars in them. This was a prosperous part of town.

The girl who came to the door was likely

around fifteen. She was tall, bony, blonde, and pretty in a flawed sort of way. She'd probably be a beauty when she got older. Right now, her thick glasses and her pimples weren't helping. And neither was the T-shirt with the ketchup stain on it. "Yes? May I help you?"

"I wondered if your father was home."

"He's in the back yard." From her right hand dangled a copy of *The Great Gatsby.* "What's your name, please?"

When I told her, she jerked back as if I'd slapped her. "Sam McCain?" Disbelief made her gulp. Her father had obviously told her all about me. "Sam McCain," she said again as if she'd just seen a spaceship land. "I'll go tell him, but I'm not sure what he's going to say."

"Oh, I've never seen your father at a loss for words yet. I'll bet he has plenty to say when you tell him."

She shrugged thin shoulders and said, "Just wait here." She paused: "This is my favorite book. I can't decide if I'm more like Daisy or more like Gatsby." Then she was gone into the shadows of the house. All the drapes had been drawn to keep the sun from scorching the interior. Somewhere a radio played "Love Me Do." Hearing the Beatles reminded me of Reverend Cartwright standing there in his burned robes. Every once in a while, justice really does prevail.

He looked sporty in the white tennis shorts and Hawaiian shirt. Even the drink in his hand looked jaunty in its tall narrow glass. He didn't open the screen door. "What the hell are you doing here?"

I saw his daughter materialize in the shadows behind him. I didn't want to insult him for her sake. "Look, I just need to ask you a few questions."

"This is neither the time nor the place. And I'd think you'd be putting together another one of your so-called peace marches. You managed to get Lou Bennett killed. Maybe next time you can get me or some other patriot killed, too."

"I want to know more about the fire that killed Karen Shanlon. You know this doesn't have anything to do with patriotism. This could be a criminal investigation."

He angled his head and said, "Nina, you go help your mother hang wash in the back yard."

She left without a word.

He said, "I've heard that you've been talking to people about it. I have a friend in the library who tells me you've been reading up on it."

I knew it wasn't Trixie Easley. She hated the chief as much as I did. She'd been one of his targets many times when he wanted to have a certain book purged from the library.

"I'm curious about it. There's no chance you could have been wrong? That it wasn't accidental after all?"

"You want to know how many diplomas I have? They signify all the courses I've taken in various aspects of being not just a chief but an inspector as well. I don't claim to know everything, but I'm not lazy. I keep up with my subject. I try to learn everything new that comes down the pike. And so my answer to your question is no, I did not make a mistake. Karen was smoking in bed. The house was old. There were a lot of books and papers around. I can't tell you why, but she didn't wake up in time. The working theory is that she was overcome by smoke before she even got out of bed. We'll never know for sure. But she did die in an accidental fire. And it was too bad. From everything I've heard about her, she was a very decent young woman."

And with that he closed the door. Didn't slam it. Just closed it quietly. I felt like an encyclopedia salesman who'd just been rejected for the sixteenth time that afternoon.

I walked back to my ragtop. Lawn mowers roared. You could smell the heat.

I'd just slid in behind the wheel when Nina came around from the back of the house and walked up to me.

"This is a neato car."

"Thanks."

"He give you grief?"

"Not really. He was probably nicer to me than I would have been to him under the circumstances." I hadn't believed him, but I wasn't going to tell her that.

"He's not my real father. My real dad died in a plane crash. He flew cargo planes."

"I'm sorry."

"I was little, but I remember him." She nodded to the house. "We don't get along very well. My mom always takes his side." Then: "I thought you were maybe the guy coming back."

"What guy?"

"The guy who came late last night. They were near the garage arguing. My bedroom window's right next to the drive. They woke me up." She ran her fingers along the chrome trim of the windshield.

"Did you see who it was?"

"Huh-uh. I got kind of scared, because he

183

said that my stepdad was going to be in trouble if he screwed this up."

"You're sure that's what he said?"

"It's *exactly* what he said, because he said it a couple of times." She buffed some dust off the hood with her fingers.

"So you didn't get a look at the other man at all?"

"He was past the point where I could see from the window. My mom takes pills. I don't think she woke up. I couldn't sleep after that. So I finally got up and went downstairs to get some milk, and my stepdad was down there. In the kitchen. Alone. He had a drink. It was a pretty strong one. I can tell by the color. It was real dark, which means he'd poured a lot in."

"He say anything to you?"

"Not much. We don't talk that much. I'm not real popular at school. That bugs him a lot more than it bugs me. I read a lot of science fiction. That's what I want to do someday. Write science fiction. You know, like Robert Heinlein."

"*Double Star*'s my favorite."

"Hey, really?" The smile made her pretty. "You really like him?"

He came around the corner armed with intent. In this case, the intent was to get me off his property and to get his stepdaughter to shut up. He was big and burly and red-faced from heat and liquor. The festive colors of the Hawaiian shirt seemed to fade.

"What the hell do you think you're doing, McCain?"

"I was just talking to him. It's my fault. He was ready to leave."

"You get inside."

He and Roy Davenport were good at ordering females inside. Leave the real business to the menfolk. Sounded like an episode of *Gunsmoke*.

"Nice to meet you, Mr. McCain."

She didn't do either of us any favors with that remark. She'd hear about it when he found her later. I was hearing about it now.

"You ever heard of jailbait, McCain?"

I laughed. I couldn't help it. "You really going to try some horseshit like that on me?"

"She's fourteen years old. That's jailbait age. That's also prison age for anybody who goes near her. She's not much to look at, but it's my duty to protect her and that's what I damned well plan to do. So how would you like it if I started telling people you've been sniffing around my innocent little stepdaughter?" The sun was turning his forehead into the texture of new leather.

"Wouldn't work, DePaul. We were talking

185

about science fiction. And she'd testify to that."

"Science fiction." His lips twisted into a particularly ugly frown. "That's why she doesn't have any friends. Sits in her room and reads that crap. No wonder other kids don't want to hang around her." He'd lost his place in the book. Now he went back to the right page. "But that doesn't make her any less vulnerable to some creep like you trying to get to her." He slammed a big hand flat on my hood. He was strong enough to dent it. I scanned the impression his hand had left in the light dust. No dent. "Now you get the hell out of here and don't try to contact her in any way. I don't ever want to see you again. Because if I do, I'm going to file a complaint against you. And how'll that look for you and that fancy-ass judge you work for? Accused of statutory rape." He was suddenly delighted with the idea. "I can see her face now when she's trying to explain it."

"It'd never stick. And she'd know better."

"It might not stick, McCain. But it'd be in the paper. And people wouldn't forget it even if the charges got dropped. Tryin' to pick up an innocent fourteen-year-old girl. See how many clients you get then."

I wanted to ask him who his late-night

visitor had been. I wanted to ask him why he was so afraid of what I'd find out about the fire and his role in assessing it. I wanted to ask if he'd taken money for his trouble, or had somebody blackmailed him into calling it an accident.

But I couldn't ask him any of these things. If I brought up his visitor, he'd know that his stepdaughter had told me. And if I asked him the other two things, he'd just sputter and stammer and threaten me.

I turned the engine on and dragged the gearshift into reverse. "I'm sure we'll be talking again sometime, Chief. Whether you want to or not."

"Try me, McCain. Try me and see what happens."

But by then I was backing up and turning on the radio. "Wooly Bully" was the perfect exit music.

I thought about my conversation with Nina DePaul as I sat across the living room from my father an hour later. He'd fallen asleep in his easy chair, his chin touching his chest, his snoring soft and gentle. Telepathy had always been one of my favorite themes in the science fiction Nina and I had discussed. The dramatic use was to pluck earth-shattering secrets from the minds of enemy agents. But what I wanted to do was share my father's life through his eyes. His early years on the farm, his father crushed in a tractor accident. His trek with his brother to Black River Falls looking for work. Their mother virtually deserting them by marrying a man who didn't want them. The worst of the Depression and then the death of his brother from influenza. Settling in a shack along the river and meeting my mother one day when she was out picking vegetables from her family's small garden. Their courtship that always sounded glamorous despite all the poverty. The years apart during the war. And the war itself that still sometimes troubled my father's sleep. And then coming back to enough prosperity to escape the Hills, only to see my brother Robert die. And now his final years, this smaller man in the old chair where he'd watched his sacred football games every Saturday and Sunday; where he'd ranted against the GOP; and where he tried to make his peace with cultural changes as different as Elvis Presley, civil rights, and yet another war.

There were times I'd resented him, times I'd even hated him, I suppose; but these times were always forgotten in the respect I had for what he'd been through and the love I felt for all the patience and encouragement and love he'd given me. Hell, I'm sure there were times when he'd hated *me.*

So I sat there now in the flurry of the fans in the windows and the faint kitchen sounds of my mother making a cold meal for this hot day and his rerun of *Maverick* playing unseen on the TV set — I sat there once again thinking the unthinkable. That he was going to die and die soon. And then I thought of my mother and my sister in Chicago and how we'd never quite be the same again.

I eased off the couch and went into the kitchen.

The way she looked at me, I knew she knew. She wiped her hands on her apron and came over to me and with a single finger dabbed away the tears on my cheek. Then she slid her arms around me and hugged me.

I went over to the refrigerator and got a can of Hamm's and sat down at the table.

"I put extra mayo in the potato salad the way you like it."

"Thanks."

She was using a wooden spoon to mix up the contents in a green glass bowl. She didn't look up when she spoke. "We want to be happy for him when we eat."

"I know."

"I try to do my crying in the morning when he takes his first nap. Isn't that crazy? It's like making an appointment. But he needs me to be happy because he's afraid."

"I know he is. I see it in his face sometimes."

"He believes, but he doesn't believe." This time she did look at me. "He's like you in that respect."

"Yeah, I guess he is."

"I wish you two could believe the way I do. Then it wouldn't be so bad. I really believe that God will take him to heaven. And I don't mean angels and harps and all that stuff. That's for children. But to a place where he'll know real peace. You know he's never gotten over his brother dying. Or *your* brother dying, either. All our lives I'd see him sitting alone sometimes, and he'd have the same kind of tears you just had in your eyes. And I always knew who he was remembering. In the days when it would get real bad with him, I'd hold him and rock him the way I used to hold you and your sister and brother. And rock you the same way. And I never felt closer to him than I did then. Because I'd never felt so needed or useful." She wrenched away without warning and moments later was sobbing into the hands covering her face.

I went over and held her. Her entire body shook. I remembered doing this when I was twelve years old. My father had fallen on the ice and cracked his skull. For several hours, the docs wondered if he'd live. I'd never seen my mother cry like that. I hadn't known what to do. I just stood still and let her cling to me. Finally I put my arms around her and patted her back the way I would pat a dog. It was stupid, the way I handled it, but I could tell it helped her.

"And here I'm the one telling you we need to be happy," she said, pulling her apron up from her waist to pat the tears from her eyes. She took a deep breath. "Potato salad and cold cuts and slices of fresh melon and iced tea. How does that sound?"

"That sounds great."

"There should be a vegetable, but he hates them as much as you do."

"I learned from the master."

"I'm going to run to the bathroom and freshen up. Would you mind setting the table, and then we'll be ready to eat?"

"Fine."

There were the everyday dishes and the special dishes. I used the former. Paper napkins, too, not the cloth ones. I used to get an extra quarter a week on my allowance if I set the table every night. I decided not to charge her this week.

When we were all set, when my mother was placing the food on the table, I went in and woke my father. Or tried to. This was one of those terrifying times when he didn't respond right away. One of those terrifying times when I was almost certain that he was dead.

But then his head raised and his eyes opened and he gazed up at me with blue eyes that were both innocent and ancient. I couldn't help myself. I leaned down and gave him an awkward hug and kissed him atop his freckled bald head.

Then we went in and ate, and he got to telling some of his favorite war stories, and the happiness my mother wanted came pure and natural to each of us. There was even laughter in the McCain household.

I was pushing open the back door when the phone rang. Wouldn't be for me. Didn't live here any more. All grown up. More or less. For her last birthday, my mother was the recipient of a yellow wall phone for the kitchen. She was as proud of that phone as I would have been of a 1939 Ford Woody. I had one foot on the rear steps when she said, "It's for you, Sam."

When I was just a few steps away she covered the phone and said, "It's a woman."

"A woman?" my father smiled. "Did you hear that, Sam?"

"It's fun to be back in seventh grade," I said. "Our little Sam has a girlfriend."

My mother swatted me on the arm and winked at my father.

"Hello."

"My mother always told me that boys didn't like girls who called them," Wendy said. "Too forward. The boys lost all respect."

"I think she was right. I'm so disgusted I'm going to hang up. By the way, we have an audience. My folks. They just told me I have to be in by ten."

"Well, I'm hoping I can keep you out a little later than that. I'd like to see you, and I also have a little bit of information about Lou Bennett you might find interesting."

"I'd like to take a shower and change clothes."

"I was thinking the same thing myself. How does eight sound?"

"Sounds just about right. I'll pick you up."

"I really enjoyed seeing you, Sam. That's all I've been thinking about all day. It's just so weird how things happen sometimes. Good things *and* bad things." Then: "By the way, let's go someplace where we can dance. It's been a long time for me."

"You don't know what you're asking for."

"Well, I'm no ballerina, so we're even up. See you at eight."

After I hung up and peeked around the kitchen door into the dining room, I saw my folks sitting there with their after-dinner coffee smiling at me. They'd seen me forlorn ever since Jane departed.

"And may a mother ask who that was?"

"Wendy Bennett."

She glanced at my father. "A cheerleader and one of the prettiest girls in the whole high school."

"Well, Mom, we're ten years out of high school, so I don't think stuff like that matters any more."

But yeah, it still did to immature guys like me. I wanted to call up all the popular boys I'd gone to high school with and say, "Guess who's got a date with Wendy tonight?" Eat your hearts out.

17

"There's a letter." I'd sketched in what I was working on. She looked fascinated.

"What kind of letter?"

"That part I don't know. All I can tell you is that when I went back to see Linda, I heard David and Roy Davenport arguing about a letter of some kind. I got the impression they couldn't find it. I was surprised Davenport was even there. Linda hates him."

We'd had small steaks and scotches and waters and a number of cigarettes. We'd said hello to a combined total of a dozen people (mine were clients, hers were friends). And we'd danced slow to a medley of Platters songs played by a house band that had been in grade school when the Platters had been popular. We'd even danced fast several times. Now we were having our second drinks, sitting in a tiny dark alcove that overlooked the dance floor.

She wore a pale-blue dress and matching one-inch heels. Her face was lightly made up and even prettier than usual. She'd always been a sort of sophisticated version of the girl next door, and adulthood had only enhanced that impression.

She was also stubborn, a quality I'd forgotten about. Not until now was she willing to go back to the brief conversation we'd had earlier about the letter.

"This letter you were telling me about two or three days ago."

"Very funny. It was just about an hour ago. You've held up pretty well for a geezer. I was afraid you might fall asleep on me."

"They were arguing about a letter."

"They sure were. Davenport said they had to get busy and find it."

Somebody looking for a letter might explain why somebody had tossed my office and Kenny's trailer, knocking out both Turk and Kenny in the process.

"Tell me about Linda's husband."

"Do I have to? This soon after eating?" She reached over and patted my hand. "Only because I'm having a good time." She sipped her scotch and said, "I read a lot of British mystery novels. They're like fantasies for me. Pure escape. Murder in all those little villages. And David fits right in there.

He's the bounder who seduces all the beautiful married women and lives off his wife's inheritance."

"You mean that literally?"

"The part about sleeping with beautiful married women? Of course. My parents are big at the country club, and they always have stories about who David is sleeping with on the side. He's even been beaten up a few times. Once badly enough to put him in the hospital for a week. Lou despised him. He always begged Linda to get rid of him. But that's the irony. You know what a snob she is. A very arrogant woman. But she's completely at the mercy of her husband. I never thought I'd feel sorry for her, but I can't help myself. It's almost as if she's deranged. Obviously she knows what he's doing. And she also knows that he practically destroyed the two small businesses Lou put him in charge of. Lou had to step in to save them from declaring bankruptcy. She could have so many men — men just as handsome but men who'd treat her the way she deserves. It's pretty sad when you see them together. The way she looks at him. It's like puppy love to the highest power. Bryce used to talk about it, too. He and David loathed each other."

"But Lou put up with him living under

the same roof?"

"Well, the north section is kind of separate from the rest of the house. You know how big the place is. Linda and David have their bedroom and study and living room over there. And their own separate entrance when they choose to use it. And they take most of their meals in the living room. The maid always makes two separate meals — excuse me, 'made' two separate meals — one for Lou because of his health, and the other one for Linda and David."

"Does David work?"

"Oh? You didn't know? He's a writer. Or says he is. He's been working on this novel for a couple of years now. He won't let anybody read it until it's finished, Linda says. I doubt it even exists."

A waitress worked her way over to our alcove. The white silk blouse and the black skirt with the large sash-like black leather belt combined with her long dark hair and exceptional height to give her a dramatic effect.

We decided on one more drink, and then Wendy said to the young woman, "I'd like to wake up some day looking like you."

The waitress had a wide TV-commercial smile. "Are you kidding? You've got those aristocratic facial bones and those beautiful eyes. I'll be happy to trade you."

"You're going to get a very nice tip out of this," I said to her. After she was gone, I said, "She's striking, but you're a lot better-looking."

"Maybe. But there're a lot of women who look like me. Young housewives. Millions of us. But she —" She picked up her cigarette, took a deep drag, and said, "Does it bother you that we're getting older?"

"Well, if we weren't getting older we'd be dead."

"That's very cute, Sam, but how about an honest answer? I wanted to do something with my life after I finished college, and I didn't. I wanted to make Bryce love me, and I didn't. I wanted to have a child, preferably a daughter, and I didn't."

"You're not exactly haggard."

"No, but I'm weary sometimes. And I'm only twenty-eight. If I'm this weary now, what'll I be like when I turn thirty-five?" Then she waved her words away. "I'm feeling sorry for myself because I've got this stupid idea that maybe we'll sleep together tonight and I want to, but I more *don't* want to."

"Then we won't."

"I haven't slept with a man in two years."

"You've dated a few. I've seen you out

sometimes."

"In the movies it's always sex sex sex, but it's never been that way with me. Maybe there's something wrong with me. I really need to feel something for the man I have in my bed."

"I'm not much for one-night stands myself."

"But I'll bet you've had some."

"What I've had — mostly — is a series of relationships that didn't work out."

"Pamela Forrest? God, I used to feel so sorry for you in high school. The way you followed her around. And Stu was such a shit to everybody. I always thought they deserved each other. I always thought you should have married Mary. She was so sweet and pretty and nice."

"Everybody thought I should've married her. But I just didn't love her the way she wanted me to — the way I should have."

"And then this last one?"

"Jane."

"I saw you a few times on the dance boat that goes downriver. I was there with one of my gentleman friends. He was quite taken with her looks. And I have to say she is a very elegant woman. Very big-city." The soft laugh. "Needless to say, I didn't invite him in for a drink."

"I'm not over her completely yet, but I'm getting there."

"Well, this should be interesting then, Sam. I'm worried about going to bed because it has to mean something to me, and you're still in love with somebody else."

"Not exactly. I'm getting over someone else. There's a difference."

The waitress returned with our drinks. We thanked her and she left.

"By the way," Wendy said. "David can be very funny — but not on purpose. He always does this he-man thing. God, I hate that. I guess he still thinks he can charm me into bed. I was very cruel to him one day. I needed to move a lot of furniture around. The neighbor I usually use had a baseball game he had to play. And by coincidence I ran into David at the supermarket. I told him about my furniture and he went all strongman on me. Seemed he *loved* moving heavy stuff around. One of his favorite things in the whole wide world. I could read his mind, of course. He had pictures of us in bed doing all sorts of things you can still get arrested for in some states. He'd slide a few chairs around and then we'd be naked and racing to my bedroom. But he didn't know what he was in for. I had heavy chairs I needed moved from the basement up to the first floor and other heavy things I needed moved from the first floor up into the attic. I kept offering to help him but he wouldn't let me. So I just sat in the family room and drank Pepsi and smoked cigarettes and watched soap operas. You should have seen him when he was done. He had a bad crimp in his back and he couldn't get his right hand to close, and I could see that his legs were shaking. I thought he was going to fall down. The last thing he had on his mind was sex. He just sort of doddered his way out to his little sports car and took off. I'm sure he didn't want me to see him when he collapsed. I laughed for days."

"You're a cruel woman."

"I'd like to think I taught him a lesson about being faithful, but I know better. He still manages to slide his arm around me every time we're in the same room. If I was Linda, I'd send him to a vet and have him neutered." Then: "Aren't I terrible? God, he was hilarious. He looked like a lame horse when he hobbled his way out to his car."

On the way back from Wendy's — a quick kiss at the door; the promise of another date tomorrow night — I realized that somebody was following me. A yellow VW bug isn't a car that lends itself to stealth, for one thing.

And neither does pulling up close and then fading back again, for a second thing. The third thing was that her engine died when she was behind me at a stoplight. I decided that this was a good time to see what she wanted.

She was grinding the key in the ignition when I knocked on her window. She rolled it down. "Evening, Pauline." I was surprised to see her without Roy Davenport. I didn't think he'd ever let his women out of his sight.

"Oh. It's you. I'm surprised to see you."

"Sure you are. I think you flooded your car. Give it a little rest and then try again but go easy on the gas. Then you can start following me again."

We were at a residential intersection that had little traffic this time of night. The windows of the small houses gleamed with TV fantasy, and it was easy to imagine that all the people watching were happy as storybook bears in their storybook homes.

Pauline wore a black blouse sheer enough to help define her nipples in their equally sheer bra. Her legs were tanned against her white shorts.

"I seen you coming out of the restaurant tonight. With that Wendy woman. I figured you'd go to her place. Because you were obviously on a date and all. I just wanted to talk to you."

"You could always try the telephone."

"I did try the telephone. I got a little tipsy and I think I dialed your number over and over."

That would explain all the calls Mrs. Goldman had told me about.

"What'd you want to talk about?"

"Stuff — I mean, I know you don't get along with Roy. And that's who I needed to talk to. Somebody who doesn't get along with Roy."

"Did you want to talk about anything special?"

She bit her lip, inhaled deeply. "I was just scared, is all."

She was still scared. "Try starting your car again. If you get it going, pull around the corner and park. You can get in my car and we'll talk."

"I'm a shitty driver."

She got it the first try. She made it around the corner and parked under the dark weight of a maple tree. I pulled in right behind her. When I'd first seen her today, she'd been careful to walk in what she apparently thought was a provocative way. She'd been doing a parody of Jayne Mansfield doing a parody of Marilyn Monroe.

But now she took small, quick steps; nervous ones.

She got in the car and opened her purse and took out a pack of cigarettes and a half-pint silver flask. The half-pint is always referred to as "the lady's model." Yes, the delicate female who needs a snort every ten minutes to get through her day as a neurosurgeon. She took a gulp's worth and then she lighted her cigarette. "I like that song."

At the moment we were hearing "Help."

"I think Paul's cute."

"Does Roy know you're out tonight?"

"Are you kidding? He'd kill me if he found out. He's got business somewhere. He said he wouldn't be back until after midnight. He was real nervous after this phone call. I'm pretty sure it was Raines he was talking to."

"David Raines? They work together?"

She snorted. "Work together? They're like peas in a pod."

"Since when?"

"Since I came to town a couple of years ago."

Davenport and Raines again. An odd pairing. But a damned interesting one.

She took a second belt from the flask. She wasn't drunk, but she would be soon if she kept up this way.

She swallowed. "If you were nicer, I'd offer you a drink." She smiled. "And maybe something else, too. You weren't at that Wendy woman's house very long. It mustn't have went too good, huh? She didn't come through?"

I liked her. She was as blunt as my six-year-old niece. "It was our first date."

"Oh. Still, you could've made out for a little while or something. There're a lot of things you can do without getting down and screwing, you know."

"I'll mention that to her the next time I see her. Now let's get back to Roy on the telephone. So, what did Roy say when he was on the phone?"

She was tamping another cigarette from her pack when she said: "Two times I heard him say something about a letter."

"Did he say anything about the letter? What it might say? Or who had it? Or anything like that?"

"He just said they needed to find the letter. He sounded pretty pissed off about it. That's all those two talk about. Everywhere we go. Roy is calling Raines or Raines is calling Roy." She frowned. "The mood he's in, he's gonna hurt me when he comes back."

"Are you really afraid he'll hurt you?"

"He already hurts me plenty. But then he always comes around and apologizes. He even cried about it once."

"You can always leave him."

"And go where? And do what? I got it made with Roy. I just want him to go back to the way he was before Lou was killed. I know you're workin' on the case, that's why I wanted to talk to you. I thought maybe I could help you."

"You've helped me a lot."

"I have?"

"You know how to get hold of me, Pauline. If you need any help, call me. All right? Night or day. I'm going to give you my card. My office number's on the front and I'll write my home number on the back." I had the feeling she hadn't told me everything she knew, but at the rate she was swilling booze she was going to be unconscious before long.

After I handed her the card and she started sliding out of the ragtop, she said, "I hope you have better luck with Wendy the next time."

She took another belt on her way to her VW.

■ ■ ■ ■

PART THREE

■ ■ ■ ■

18

I wondered what a suitable time would be for visiting David Raines. I hadn't slept well. Pauline's stories kept waking me up. I studied them as if I was doing an autopsy. Raines and Davenport working together on something. And upset about a letter.

I ate breakfast at the café near the courthouse. The fans were already going. Ninety-four was the prediction for this afternoon. It was already seventy-eight.

All the tables and booths were taken. I sat at the counter between a slurper and a guy who kept talking to me with his mouth full of sausage. It was like looking at the innards of road kill. The slurper was eventually replaced by an enormous man who giggled as he read the funnies. "Boy, that Dagwood sure gets in some trouble, don't he?" The other guy ordered more sausages. "That Beetle Bailey, he sure cracks me up." I paid mesmerized attention to the newspaper, hoping he'd leave me alone.

Molly had written another story about Lou Bennett's death. Between the lines, you could hear her throbbing heart beating out a romantic rhythm. Not many murder suspects were called "strikingly handsome" or "eloquent" or "courtly." She twice implied that with Cliffie's track record, there were "some unnamed sources" who were convinced of Doran's innocence.

The general café conversations ran to how the Hawkeye football team was shaping up for the fall and whether the Cubs could come back. Standard stuff. I kept glancing at the clock with the cracked face above the three coffeepots. It was only seven thirty. I'd decided to wait until eight thirty to show up at the Bennett estate.

I was just coming back from the john when somebody shouted: "Rachel, turn on the radio!"

The jukebox had been playing an old Connie Francis song, "Where the Boys Are." Somebody jerked the plug from its socket-ending Connie's phrase half-sung.

Rachel dialed around until she found what everybody was waiting to hear. "To repeat: the body of Black River Falls resident Roy Davenport was found in his garage early this morning by a close female friend. Police

Chief Sykes said that Davenport had been shot three times. Sykes also said that he's reasonably sure foul play was involved."

Laughter rattled all the glassware. That's how you wanted your day to start — a good laugh at Cliffie's incompetence. "Reasonably sure foul play was involved." Poor dumb Cliffie.

But past the joke was the reality of Davenport's murder. Lou Bennett and now his former business partner. And something about a letter. What the hell was going on?

I walked up to the cash register and paid my bill. Then I went outside and stood smoking a cigarette and watching the town come alive. The milkmen were finishing the last of their rounds in their white trucks, the mailmen in their summer shorts and short-sleeved shirts were just beginning theirs. The kids who played on baseball teams were headed out to Kilmead Park, where the city had recently taken some old bleachers from one of the high schools and set them down next to the ball diamond to give the parents a place to sit while watching their offspring play in T-shirts provided by the businesses that sponsored them. Then there were the young mothers pushing strollers, doing some light shopping before the heat got worse.

I was trying to decide where I'd learn more. I needed to talk to Pauline. The problem was that Cliffie would have her stuck in a room somewhere, shouting questions at her. He would be shocked that she and Davenport had been living in sin. It would be best to keep with my original plan. David Raines would no doubt be coming apart. Davenport's murder likely had something to do with the mysterious letter and whatever the two men had been involved in.

On the drive out, I realized that the discovery of Davenport's body would make a good case for Harrison Doran. Lou Bennett and now Roy Davenport, both murdered. Obviously there was a connection, and even Cliffie would have to see it. Much as Doran didn't want to leave jail, he'd soon be walking free again.

A man in a gray uniform was working the lawn with a power mower. A truck with the words LAWN KINGS was parked off the asphalt drive. The mower sounded angry in the morning stillness.

I pulled up to the front steps and parked. Somebody had been watching me from a second-floor window. I saw a blur of flesh and then a curtain falling back in place. I went up to the door and used a brass knocker the size of a catcher's mitt to announce my presence.

I don't know who I was expecting to see when the massive door opened, but it wasn't William Hughes. His dark skin contrasted well with his red summer shirt and white ducks. He didn't look happy to see me.

"Is there something I can do for you, Mr. McCain?"

"I'd like to see David Raines."

"Neither Mr. nor Mrs. Raines is seeing anybody today."

"Having sex all day, are they?"

"I've got things to do. And I'm sure you do too. So let's not waste any more time. I'll tell David that you called. He may get back to you. Good day, Mr. McCain."

"Who is it, William?"

I watched her emerge from the deep morning shadows that cast the staircase into brooding relief. She wore an outfit of puce sleeveless blouse and matching walking shorts. White Keds covered her feet.

She saw me before William spoke my name.

"It's all right, William. I'll talk to him."

"He asked for David."

"I'll handle it, William." She drew up next to him and touched his arm in an affectionate way. "It'll be all right."

He looked at me and smiled. "You finally

won one, McCain."

"My lucky day, I guess."

"Luck has a way of running out." He returned her touch. "Just be careful, Linda. He likes to think he's tricky, and sometimes he is."

As his footsteps retreated, she said, "You two know each other. It's one surprise after another this morning."

"Meaning Roy Davenport?"

The lovely face tightened. "Maybe you can help me — or help my husband, I should say. William said that you wanted to talk to David anyway. He's on the veranda having coffee." She paused. "He won't be happy to see you. He'll barely speak to me. He's obviously in some kind of trouble. I'm sure you've heard all the gossip about the differences we've had in our marriage. What nobody ever says is that I still love my husband very much. And I want to help him."

She didn't wait for my answer. She blazed a trail through the house to a flagstone veranda where Raines sat beneath an umbrella'd table overlooking the exquisite green grounds of the estate. The drink in front of him was dark with bourbon.

"What the hell's he doing here?" he said when we approached the table.

"I asked him to talk to you — since you won't talk to me. I'm afraid for you."

"And this bastard's going to help me? God, Linda, use your brain for once." His face was red from drink and his eyes pinched and pink from lack of sleep. "I've already told you this is something I can handle. Roy's dead. Don't I have a right to be shocked?"

"Yes, of course. But there's something you're not telling me."

I didn't want to slog through the soap opera any longer. "I wanted to ask you about a certain letter, Raines. That's why I came out here. Somebody I know heard you and Davenport arguing about it one night."

He surprised me. Instead of fury he tried scorn. "Did Pauline take care of you while you were with her? I'll bet she's taken care of enough men to fill a football stadium."

"David, there's no need to be vulgar."

"Well, it's true. I could never figure out why Roy kept that slut around anyway."

It was still somewhat cool out here. The robins and jays and sparrows in the trees sang sweet and loud. And to the east I could see the quarter horses run inside the fenced-in land Lou Bennett used for his animals. Be nice to just sit here and read and doze off in one of the comfortable lounge chairs scattered across the veranda.

"Are we finished now, McCain? You came out here ready to scare me with some bullshit Pauline told you. I'm sorry she didn't come through for you. Roy said she's quite good."

"For God's sake, David. Have some respect for me if you don't have any for yourself."

"Oh, don't worry. This is the kind of talk McCain here traffics in. He's a cheap little lawyer in a cheap little business. Ask any of the established men in this town. He's a joke and I don't want him dirtying up our home."

Enjoy it while you can, asshole, I thought. I didn't want to embarrass Linda Raines any more than she was already. But someday I'd have my shot at him. Someday soon.

"Why don't you show me out, Mrs. Raines?"

"Yes, of course."

"The judge has lost several friends because of you, McCain. They're afraid she'll pick up your stench some day and give it to them. I can smell it on the air already." He addressed this to the glass in his hand rather than to me.

Linda Raines had tears in her eyes. This time I didn't trail her. This time she slid her arm through mine and led me through the house as if I'd been wounded. But she was the one who'd been hurt, and I suspected she'd been hurt many times before.

"He isn't really mean. He just has moods. I'm so sorry."

"That's all right."

"Were you serious about this letter?"

No point in frightening her even more. "Maybe he's right. Maybe it's just a story. Pauline does like to drink a lot."

"I've been around them a few times, Roy and her. She's not my type, but I felt sorry for her, the way she's treated. Roy certainly didn't mind humiliating her in front of other people." I don't think she caught the irony of her own words.

At the door she said, "The lawyers we know here, they're all David's friends. If I ever needed advice —"

I found a card and scribbled my home phone on the back. I handed it to her. "I'd put this where David can't find it. I don't think he'd be very happy about it."

"No," she said, her beauty momentarily ruined by worry and confusion. "No, but then there are a lot of things David isn't very happy about."

Lynn Shanlon was carrying groceries from

her Dodge station wagon to the stoop in back of her house. When I pulled into her drive, she had a quick smile for me and then kept on with her work. Being a gentleman of the old school — at least when it didn't take too much energy on my part — I grabbed the last two sacks and carried them to the stoop myself.

"I'll be happy to give you a hand getting them inside."

"That's all right. I have to lock Grace in her room first. She's the little gray cat. She always tries to get outside. I get tired of seeing my pets hit by cars, so I don't let them out any more. If I keep opening the back door, Grace'll be out of here in a flash." She pointed to the top step, where there was room enough for two adults to park themselves. "You want to sit down and have a cigarette while I get us some coffee?"

"Sure. You do your grocery shopping pretty early, don't you?"

"This way, I beat the crowds. Lots of things on sale today. This is what you do when you work at the courthouse and have a mortgage to pay off. I'll be right back."

Her tidy blue skirt allowed me a closer look at her comely legs with all their freckles. The white blouse draped her small sweet breasts. She watched me watch her for a moment and smiled. Before she went inside, she mussed my hair and said, "You men. That's all you ever think about, isn't it?" Then: "Well, at least you're cute. You should see some of the mastodons that come after me."

"Mastodons" kept me amused the whole time she was gone. And as she handed me my mug, she said, "So what's so funny?"

" 'Mastodons.' "

"Oh, right." She sat down next to me on the step. "Karen and I saw this movie when we were young called *The Beast from 20,000 Fathoms*. It was supposed to be a horror movie, but we both felt sorry for the beast when they killed him at the end. I guess we sort of identified with him. We always considered ourselves sort of freaks. I had really terrible complexion problems, and poor Karen had her limp. But anyway, after we saw that movie we both got interested in dinosaurs. We were told it was very unlady-like, but we didn't care. We gobbled up everything we could find. So mastodons and creatures like that became part of our normal vocabulary." She laughed. "God, did *that* sound dumb. Pretty interesting conversation to listen to, right?"

"Very interesting, actually. Two pretty

young girls becoming fascinated with dinosaurs."

"Oh, we weren't pretty, believe me. Not to ourselves, anyway. We really thought we were homely. We didn't even have a soda shop date until we were well into high school. My folks took me to Iowa City, where this doctor really helped me with my complexion. And by that time, Karen was so beautiful even she had to admit it to herself. I'm pretty enough, I suppose, but I'm plain compared to my sister." Then: "God, I miss her. There isn't a day goes by that I don't think about her and kind of talk to her."

"Did she ever mention a certain letter to you? It probably had something to do with Roy Davenport or David Raines."

Over the picket fence in the back yard, a bald man called out Lynn's name and waved. She waved back. The man dipped down and moments later a power mower roared to life. "That's Mr. Nelson. He's a very good neighbor. Unlike the old bitch down the street. You represented her, remember? Against me?"

"You ever forget that? This is the second time you brought it up."

She smiled. "I'm just kidding you. But she really is an old bitch, and Mr. Nelson and his wife are really very nice people. And no, I don't know anything about a letter. Why are you interested in it?"

"Because Roy Davenport was interested in it. And so is Raines."

"All I know about Roy Davenport is that Karen and I were afraid of him. We'd heard all the rumors. I shouldn't be speaking ill of the dead, but we were always told that he had a record and that Lou had hired him to do his dirty work. Lou didn't want to spoil his image, you know. But it was fine with him if Davenport did things. Karen got a threatening phone call one night. About seeing Bryce. The man said that something bad would happen to her if she didn't stop seeing him. She was convinced it was Davenport, that he'd just muffled his voice somehow."

"Did you tell this to Cliffie?"

"Now, what do you think? Of course I did. But what good did it do me? He said it was probably a prank call. And he said that my information was hearsay since I hadn't heard the call myself. So we just dropped the subject."

"How long between the phone call and the fire?"

"That was another thing. Several months."

"And that was the only call Karen told

you about?"

"Yes."

"And there weren't any other threats?"

"Not threats like that. Just the usual from the family to Bryce, and then Bryce would tell Karen about them. And I shouldn't say 'threats' as such. They were really warnings about how Bryce was screwing up his life. Which meant that he was screwing up Lou's life. Lou wanted royal blood in the family line. Or what he considered royal blood, anyway. Which is funny when you think about it. How much royal blood is there in Black River Falls?"

"Well, there are a few people who think they're royalty, so I suppose that could pass for the real thing." I set my mug down and eased myself up. I could see the back yards of several houses. White houses and white garages against green grass and yellow and orange and pink lilies and various other flowers. A man in a straw hat and a pipe in his mouth leaned against a fence talking to a neighbor. It all looked like a Norman Rockwell painting for a *Saturday Evening Post* cover.

"I wish somebody had tried to warn me off my ex the way Lou tried to warn Bryce off Karen."

She'd never explained the reason for her

split with the Chicago banker, but it was clear she wasn't over it. She was bound to him by love or hate, it was hard to tell. Maybe both.

"If you think of anything else, I'd appreciate a call."

"I feel sorry for that poor dumb Pauline. She's sweet, in a weird way. I wonder what's going to happen to her."

"Yeah," I said as I started to leave. "I'll bet she's wondering the same thing."

19

"So you have no idea what's in this letter?"

"No."

"What do you *think* might be in it?"

"Since when are you interested in speculation?"

That earned me a rubber band fired from the slender hand of Judge Esme Anne Whitney. Perched on her desk in a light-gray linen suit with matching pumps, Her Honor was firing at an angle and she missed. Which was why I'd taken the chair farthest away from her.

"It's hardly speculation. We have two people dead. And you've been doing research on the fire that killed Karen Shanlon. So unless you're completely wasting your time and mine, you see a connection between the two."

"Fair enough. But I still have no idea what's in the letter."

"But you're thinking it bears on the fire."

"Maybe. But then again, who knows. The more I find out about your esteemed friend Lou Bennett, the more I realize that he had a lot of questionable business interests. There's always the possibility that the fire had nothing to do with these deaths. Bennett and Davenport were in business together. Maybe they made somebody very angry. One of the people I talked to told me that Davenport had been hired because he was muscle. If Bennett needed muscle, he could have been involved in just about anything."

I was enjoying the courthouse air conditioning. Balmy electric breezes made me want to close my eyes and sleep. But then I felt selfish. Not only did I have to deal with this case, I also had to deal with my father. I was bitching about losing sleep; he was facing death. And my mother was facing a kind of death of her own.

"I have to admit I envy you the privilege of seeing David Raines afraid. He's one of those people who always sweeps into a room and takes over. He was amusing the first few times I invited him to my parties. But between chasing after half the wives there and patting me on the behind, I got tired of him very quickly."

I laughed. I knew I shouldn't laugh. I tried

not to laugh. But I couldn't help myself. The image of *anybody* patting the Ice Maiden on her "behind" was hilarious. I'm surprised she didn't pull out a gun (she has several) and kill him on the spot.

"Go ahead and laugh, McCain. That's your sordid little world, not mine. All four of my husbands had their flaws, but they were all gentlemen and behaved accordingly. And you'd damned well better never share that story with anybody, do you understand?" For a striking woman of noble bones, she had the ability to suddenly turn into Joseph Stalin when she threatened you.

"DePaul interests me, too. He was the one who signed off on the fire. Said it was an accident."

"And why would he do that?"

"Money, why else? I have a call in to a friend at the credit bureau. The bank won't help me because I don't have a badge. But this woman will because we're old friends."

"I'm sure you're sleeping with her or have slept with her or plan to sleep with her, and I don't want to hear anything about it."

"Believe it or not, we're just friends. She's happily married to a very nice guy. But I've known her since we went to grade school together."

"Oh, yes. That Catholic school."

As a good patrician, Judge Whitney is of the belief that papists, if they had any couth and courage, would be Episcopalians. A certain harshness comes into her voice when she pronounces the word "Catholic."

"So it's completely innocent. I *do* have women friends who are just that."

She sighed and slid off the desk. She walked behind her desk and sat down and picked up the phone. She dialed without hesitation and then said, "John, it's Esme. I'm about to ask you something that you can never share with anybody. I'd like copies of Ralph DePaul's banking records for the past five years. Xerox copies. And at the moment I can't explain why."

No amenities; no small talk. John could only be John K. Bridges, president of First National.

Whatever he said took less than a minute. She said: "Thank you, John. If you would have somebody bring them to my chambers as soon as possible, I'd appreciate it. Will I see you on the links tomorrow?" Pause. "Good. I'll be breaking in my new clubs. Thank you very much again, John." She hung up.

"Wow. You must really have something good on him."

"I wish you'd stop thinking like a criminal

someday, McCain. We're friends. Why wouldn't he help me?"

"Well, let's see. At the least, what he's doing is unethical, and at the worst it's criminal. A good lawyer could make a strong case against him."

"Well, I'm safe there. I don't *know* any good lawyers; do you?"

"Present company excepted, of course."

"Call me early this afternoon. I'll have the information for you then. And it'll be a lot more useful than anything you'll get from the credit bureau."

Her phone rang. She brushed me away with her left hand as she lifted the receiver with her right.

I had been banished from the hothouse garden of Esme Anne Whitney.

As I came down the steps of the courthouse, I saw an attorney named Aaron Farmer talking to a man in a wheelchair. Farmer was just saying good-bye. His briefcase swinging, he ran up the steps I'd just descended. He was from the largest firm in town. They'd never forgiven me for winning three cases from them over the years. He didn't have time to give me the full-tilt scowl — there was an official one that all the firm's lawyers used — he just gave me an Elvis; you know, that curled lip. And then continued racing up the stairs.

By now, the man in the wheelchair had swung around and watched me walk toward him. His name was Mike Parnell. We'd gone through both Catholic and public schools together. We'd never been close friends, but we'd hung out together from time to time, the most notable moment we'd shared being when both our dates at a kegger spent most of the night throwing up. We'd ended up shooting craps by the campfire.

Mike had gone into the Army straight out of high school. In 1963, he found himself in a place called Vietnam. He stepped on a land mine the day of his twenty-sixth birthday. People here always told him God gave him the greatest gift of all, life. But his eyes said differently. In them you could see both the physical pain and the psychic pain that came from losing both his legs.

Today he wore a Superman T-shirt and an angry face. He's never had much trouble with girls. He had one of those altar-boy faces that a certain kind of woman takes to immediately. There had been one exception, the girl he'd been engaged to. She deserted him after he came home. Or maybe I was being too judgmental. Mike had always had a temper — I could remember a couple of fistfights we'd had, neither of us tough or savvy, but mad enough to put on a show for our friends — so maybe it was Mike's fault. Maybe he'd made it impossible for her to stay with him.

"Sorry I didn't make it to your rally the other night, McCain."

"You didn't miss much."

"That's not what I heard. I heard you and all your friends and that faggot Doran were saying shit about the troops. And that would include me."

"Nobody said anything bad about the troops, Mike. All we said is that we don't want any more deaths because this war isn't worth it. We're on *your* side."

"Bullshit, you son of a bitch, you and your faggot friends aren't on my side." He was loud enough to attract attention. "I lose my legs over there and you're telling me I did it for nothing? That all my buddies who died over there died for nothing?" He was shouting at me now.

I was embarrassed; but even more I was ashamed, because I didn't have the right words to say to him. Maybe there *were* no right words. I felt miserable for him and the life ahead of him. And the life he'd lost on some miserable goddamn jungle trail in some miserable shit-hole of a country named Vietnam. I wanted to tell him how sorry I was for him and how I'd do anything I could to help him and how I hoped he would some day understand why we'd had the rally, why we believed as we did. But there were no words, not the right words, anyway, so I stood there in the blazing sun as people slowed to listen to him screaming at me, terrible words from a lost scared man some Dr. Strangelove general and some bought-and-paid-for politician had decided to send to yet another war.

I wanted to move away, but I couldn't. Maybe I felt I had this kind of abuse coming. It was small payment, considering the payment he'd had to make.

His words came with such violence and speed that I no longer heard them. I just stared at the sad enraged face they were coming from, remembering him when we were young and the night we shot craps by the campfire and how he was always cruising the night in his '55 black Chevy. Only to end up like this for no reason at all.

And then somebody had my hand and was tugging me away and three or four other people started shouting at me, too, joining Mike. I was several long feet away from them before I said, "Thanks." Then I slipped my hand from hers.

"No PDA, huh?"

"What's PDA?"

"God, Sam, somebody's got to sit you down and explain the facts of girl life. Public Displays of Affection."

"Oh, yeah, right."

"I don't know who I felt sorrier for, Mike or you. Both of you, I guess."

Wendy wore a starched mauve blouse and tan walking shorts. The sandals only emphasized how small her feet were, fine delicate bones beneath the ornate clutches of the sandals.

"I stopped by your office. Jamie — is that it, Jamie? — she told me you were at the courthouse. I thought I'd find you and let you buy me a cup of coffee."

"That's damned nice of you."

"I thought so too. But that seems to be my nature. Nice."

"Uh-huh. I remember that from high school."

"I wasn't *that* stuck up."

"The hell you weren't."

"Well, but then I took a sacred vow of niceness and look at me now."

"Major improvement, I'll give you that."

"Oh, look. Isn't that that little street café everybody likes so much?"

"You must have taken a sacred vow of

subtlety, too."

"You rarely get what you don't ask for. I grew up with two sisters who were both better-looking and a lot smarter than I was. I only got things when I badgered my mother for them. Subtlety gets you nowhere, Sam."

I had iced coffee, she had regular. We sat at a small table on the sidewalk under an umbrella.

Between the heat and humidity, the crowds moved slowly, as if they were under water. I watched as a meter maid put a ticket under a windshield wiper. She jerked her hand away. The windshield had been damned hot.

"I actually wanted to see you for two reasons. First, I wanted to make sure that I was going to see you tonight."

"I'm hoping so, Wendy. I had a good time last night."

"And second, from the little you told me at dinner about Lou Bennett and the fire and everything, I had an idea. Do you remember Doris Crachett?"

"Vaguely. She was a year ahead of us, right?"

"Two years, actually. We knew each other from summers at the country club. If you think *I* was a snob, you should have hung around Doris. Anyway, her father was the assistant fire chief up until a year ago. He retired then. Doris always said that Chief DePaul did too many favors for people."

"What kind of favors?"

"Well, I remember Doris said that one of the mayor's friends had a business that burned down. Her father thought it was obviously arson, but the chief wrote the report and called it accidental."

"Why didn't her father say something?"

She shrugged. "I guess he was always careful about not wanting to come on too strong — you know, with his education and his money. A lot of people made fun of him because he was a member of the country club."

"How can an assistant fire chief afford the country club?"

"Oh, they had inherited money from her father's side. Her dad had a college degree and no interest in anything special. Doris always said that he became a fireman by default. Probably thought it was exciting. He's a widower now, and he lives with Doris and her husband. The husband's a neuro-surgeon in Cedar Rapids."

"That's good to know about DePaul. That he took a dive for somebody before Karen died."

"So you owe me a dinner."

"That's how this works, huh?"

"Damn right. That's another thing you learn when you have two older sisters who are prettier and brighter than you are. You have to keep doing favors for people so they'll do a few for you."

I looked at the golden down on the slender arm and then at the curve of the long neck as she turned in profile to pick up her pack of Viceroys. Then I had a brief jolt of Jane. My first brief jolt of the day, and I'd been up for several hours. The patient seems to be doing better today, Doctor.

"So, what time are you picking me up tonight? Barring unforeseen problems of course."

"Seven."

"What would you think about The Eyrie, that new place out on the highway? We can dance there, too."

"You and dancing."

"Face it, Sam. You like it too. You just have to be all boy about it and pretend you don't. You were grinning when you were doing the Watusi."

"I was doing the Watusi? I was just sort of jerking around."

"That's what everybody does when they do the Watusi."

"Man, talk about useless information."

She laughed. "Yes, and there's a lot more where that came from." Then she tapped me on the top of my hand. "You feeling any better about Mike?"

"No. And I doubt I will. He thinks we're betraying him. It's hard to face him. I don't blame him for thinking what he does. I'd probably feel the same way if I'd gone through what he did. And here I am all safe and sound, talking against the military. I feel like shit about it."

"But you won't stop?"

"No. No, I can't. And who knows, I may have to go some day."

"You're kidding."

"No. I'm in the National Guard. I spent two weeks in June at camp. If the war keeps expanding, they'll be calling us up."

"Will you go if they do?"

"Probably. I'm not any better than the rest of the guys in my unit. We're all pretty good friends. I couldn't do that to them."

She sank back in her chair. "So the best husband material I've run across in the last two years is going to run away?"

"Write your congressman."

"You're damned right I will." Then: "Oh, shit, if you'll pardon my French. I don't want you to go. I'm already having all these stupid dreams about you — about us. Based on one night. How's that for crazy?"

"I had one or two dreams like that myself. Based on one night. Maybe it's just that we're so comfortable with each other. Maybe all that time we spent sitting next to each other in high school is finally paying off."

"I hope so. I just want to feel as good as I did last night. And as soon as I saw you this morning, I felt good again — until you brought up the war. Now I'm nervous about it."

I left a dollar tip for the waitress and stood up.

She worked her way over to me and kissed me on the cheek. "Lou wanted me to be a perfect little wife, so he made me get into all these clubs for the snooty people. I have to go to one of the meetings this afternoon."

"My kind of folks."

"I'll bet, wise-ass. So, where're you headed?"

"To talk to Cliffie, if he's back from Roy Davenport's yet."

"Sometimes I almost feel sorry for him. He's got that poor little girl with spina bifida, and when you see them together he's so loving and proud of her. But then he's so stupid at his job. Then I don't feel sorry for him, because he shouldn't be the chief. If his father hadn't bullied the city council into giving it to him, he'd be walking a beat."

I kissed her back on the cheek. "You think he knows how to Watusi?"

She jabbed me in the ribs and then we parted.

20

The lobby of the police station was filled with reporters. Two murders in a few days brought TV, radio, and print journalists from Cedar Rapids, Des Moines, Iowa City, and two or three smaller towns, in addition to our own people.

Molly was one of them. In her pink dress, sandals, and ponytail, she was the belle of this particular ball, the only other female being a surly woman from a nearby newspaper. Over beers one night, the woman told me she'd been hired to edit the paper and do rewrite. She did not like being sent out on assignment. She had a cigarette hack, could drink most men under the table, and one night belted a TV reporter who insulted the Chicago Bears. I'd considered asking her to marry me, but then I thought better of it. She was not only tougher than I was; she was also meaner.

Molly took me by the elbow and led me

into a corner perfect for whispering.

"What's wrong?" I said.

"This. Roy Davenport being murdered. Now Cliffie'll probably let Harrison go."

After all the coffee I'd had, I was self-conscious about my breath. We had to be almost head-to-head to speak in whispers. I talked out of the side of my mouth like Bogart so I wouldn't scorch her with a full blast.

"Why're you talking like that?"

"Coffee breath."

"Here, for God's sake."

She gave me a stick of Doublemint. I didn't have the heart to complain that this gum was at least as old as I was. I jammed it into my mouth and crunched down on it with my molars. It sounded like tiny rocks being crushed. Then I started whispering again. "Cliffie has to let him go. It's obvious these two murders are related. He won't have any choice."

She stamped her foot. Some of the other reporters started watching us. She whispered, "But Harrison says he needs at least a week in prison or it'll spoil the book."

"First of all, it isn't 'prison,' it's jail. Second of all, his book is a fantasy. Third of all, I can't believe you're being sucked into this."

"God, McCain. You're just so jealous, it's embarrassing."

"Not jealous, Molly. Just worried about you a little." Apparently my voice had risen, because two or three reporters started watching us again. "I don't want to see you get hurt. Doran isn't exactly stable."

"And you are? All the women you've been with, and you're not married yet? How stable is that?"

"I'm just trying to help you, Molly. That's all."

There wasn't anything else to say. I walked away. My friend Marjorie Kincaid was behind the desk again. Her black beehive hairdo was intact. I wondered how she slept with it. Maybe she had some kind of aluminum tube that slipped over it at night to keep it from getting messed up.

"Finally I get to talk to somebody who's not a reporter." She obviously didn't care if they heard her.

"Is the chief in?"

" 'The chief'? This must be very serious, Sam."

"I just want him to know how much I respect him."

"We all want him to know that, Sam. That's the reason I live."

243

"He's going to hear you one of these days."

"All the stuff I have on him — I'm not worried." She swiveled to her intercom: "Chief, Sam McCain would like to talk to you for a few minutes."

"Is he sober?"

The reporters laughed. Cliffie knew they could hear him.

"Has he grown any, or does he still look like a kid?"

Marjorie rolled her eyes. "Should I send him back?"

"I'm giving him five minutes."

She clicked off. A reporter snapped: "Why does he get to see the chief when we don't?"

"They go to the same church," Marjorie said.

"What's the denomination?"

"Druid," I said and walked back.

Cliffie was smiling when I walked into his photo gallery that he called an office. Cliffie had signed black-and-white photos from a few famous people, but mostly from people who were political hacks like himself. Famous or not, they all got framed space on his walls. Most of the poses were the same, too, Cliffie shaking hands with the person. Cliffie looked like a used-car salesman who had just unloaded the biggest lemon on the lot.

I started to sit down, but he waggled a metronome finger at me — back and forth, forth and back. "Huh-uh, McCain. You're not going to be here long enough to make it worth your while to sit down."

"You don't even know what I'm going to say."

On the wall behind him, to the right of the large window, was his most sacred framed photo, that of actor Glenn Ford.

"Oh, I know what you're going to say, McCain. When I was out there at Davenport's looking at the body I said to myself, I'll bet McCain's going to try and tell me that Lou Bennett's murder is tied to this one. That's what you're going to tell me, right?"

"Well, I —"

He held up a pudgy hand. "And then I said to myself, what he's after is to spring this Harrison Doran. He's going to say that since these two murders are tied together, Doran should be let go."

"You're making my case for me."

"Uh-uh. I'm making my case for *me*. An amateur like you sees a connection between the two killings, but an old pro like myself — huh-uh. Roy Davenport was a hood. He had plenty of enemies of his own. Whoever

killed him figured by bumping off Davenport now, it'd look like it had something to
do with the Bennett murder. Pretty good
thinking except for one thing. He hadn't
counted on a brain like mine." He tapped
his temple for dramatic effect. "You see
what I'm trying to say here, McCain? He
thinks he's outsmarting me, but I'm outsmarting him."

"With your brain."

"That's right, McCain, with my brain. So
your boy Doran stays right where he is. He
killed Lou Bennett. That one I've got
wrapped up. Now I have to start a separate
investigation to find the man who killed
Davenport. That's how an old pro does it.
Stick around. You could learn something."

"Oh, I've learned something already."

"Oh, yeah, what's that?"

"You're even dumber than I thought you
were. The same person killed Bennett and
Davenport. They were business partners for
years. If one of them had an enemy, then
the other one had the same enemy. And that
means that Doran didn't kill Bennett.
Somebody else did."

All he had for me was a contrived smile.
"Doesn't feel good, does it, McCain? I
figured this one out and you didn't. You
won't have bragging rights on this one."

"Does that mean that you know who killed Roy Davenport?"

He kept the smile. He made it wide and irritating. "Now, you don't think I'd tell *you*, do you? I'm a sworn officer of the law."

"I guess I was wrong."

That got his attention. "What? Wrong about what?"

"I just told somebody waiting to see you that even you wouldn't be stupid enough to think these murders weren't committed by the same person."

At least I got rid of his smile. "You tell a lot of people I'm stupid. And you've *been* telling them since you hung out your shingle. And you know what? I'm still chief of police and you're still a failure as a lawyer. You want to hear what some of the *successful* lawyers say about you?"

"I could give a shit what they say."

"Now that's a lie and you know it." He looked right at me. "Any more than if I was to say that I don't give a shit about some of the things you say about *me*."

I wanted to say something smart, but his honesty surprised me. He was admitting that all the scorn hurt him. He had no right to tell me this, because, at least for the moment here, I had to feel bad about making fun of him all the time. Cliffie was supposed to be a cartoon. It pissed me off that he'd forced me to see him as a human being.

Then he did me the favor of reverting to type. "It's my turn here, McCain. My turn. I'm going to solve two murders at the same time. And all the people who make fun of me behind my back will have to eat a big barrelful of shit. Hot steamy shit. And I'll guarantee you, I won't have just one killer, I'll have two. And whether you like it or not, I've already got the mouthy bastard who murdered Lou. He's sitting in a cell right down the hall there."

"He didn't do it. I don't like him much better than you do. I wish he'd never come to town, and I can barely stand to be around him for more than a minute or two. But he didn't kill Bennett. That much I'm sure of. And I don't care if you 'win' this one or not, Chief. It probably *is* your turn. All I want is to see that the right man goes to prison."

"He should be going to the gallows. But thanks to you and your liberal friends, we don't have capital punishment in this state any more." Then: "What's so funny?"

I hadn't realized I was smiling. "Just the way you manage to give little political speeches every chance you get. I know how you feel about the death penalty. You rag me about it all the time." What I'd really been smiling about was how good it felt to return to our usual adversarial relationship. He'd only gone human on me for less than thirty seconds. That amount of time I could handle. But not any more.

I walked to the door. "You'd better get out there and talk to them. They're getting restless."

"If I had my way, we'd shoot every reporter in the state on sight."

"Be sure to mention that when you're talking to them."

"You know, McCain, someday if I'm real lucky I'll be a cool guy just like you think you are."

"That's right, Chief," I said. "If you're lucky."

I didn't talk to Molly on my way out of the station. I just waved and hurried on. I didn't want to be around when she learned that Doran was not going to be released.

"I guess I don't understand, Mr. C."

In her berry-red miniskirt and white blouse, Jamie was a decided distraction. She seemed to have become even more carelessly erotic since her eighteenth birthday. Or maybe that was because I could now legally look at her as a woman. She was stretching to put a law book on the third shelf above our tiny refrigerator. The position outlined her body all too well.

"What I meant was, I'm happy to give you an advance if it's for you. Something you need or your family needs. But I'm pretty sure this is for Turk, isn't it?"

She shoved the book back on the shelf, then ended her stretch. She faced me. "He really needs this outfit. He's pretty sure a big record producer's going to be in the audience." She walked over and sat down at her desk.

"He was sure there was going to be a big record producer the last time he played this bar."

"Well, like he says, this producer is real busy. He has a lot of big stars to worry about. Sometimes he can't get away."

I wanted to point out the obvious to this girl-woman-child. I wanted to say that no record producer would ever be found checking out a bar band in Black River Falls, Iowa. I wanted to say that either Turk was living in a fantasy world or he was creating a fantasy for Jamie as a means of prying more money out of her for his "outfits." But I couldn't, because she wouldn't believe me. And because she might very well start crying. I did not need any tears on this particular morning.

"Tell you what, Jamie. How about Turk going halvsies?"

"What's 'halvesies' mean?"

"You pay half and he pays half."

"But he doesn't have any money, Mr. C."

"Well, doesn't he get paid for these gigs? He must earn *some*thing."

"Well, he earns a little bit. They have to split it up between four guys, remember. But he needs that for cigarettes and beer and stuff like that."

"Are you keeping track of how much he's borrowed from you?"

"Oh, he's not borrowing, Mr. C. I'm just giving him the money. When he gets his record deal and the money starts coming in, it's like Turk says. We'll get married and then he'll make sure I get paid back every cent."

"But you're not keeping track of what you give him. How will you know how much —" I stopped myself. Pointless to go on. "You've already borrowed against your next check, Jamie."

"He really needed those new boots. They're like the Beatles wear. Turk said people wouldn't take him serious if he didn't have boots like that. Record producers can always tell if you're up to date, Turk says."

"All right. I'll tell you what. I'm going to give you your full paycheck. We'll call what you've borrowed a bonus, all right?"

"Gosh, thanks, Mr. C."

"But there's a catch."

"There is?" She was suddenly a little girl afraid of hearing some imminent bad news. "Like what?"

"Like you won't give more than twenty percent of your check to Turk."

"How much will that be?"

"It doesn't matter. We'll figure it out. But I want you to make that agreement with me. No more than twenty percent. And that goes for every check I give you."

"I'm sorry, Mr. C, but I don't think Turk'll like that."

"Fine. Tell him to come and see me."

Her cheeks bloomed pink. "Well, I don't think you'll want to see him after you get the letter."

"What letter?"

She folded her hands and sat up straight. I'd never seen eyes cower before, but that's exactly what her eyes were doing. Cowering. "You know Mr. Dodsworth?"

"John Dodsworth, the lawyer here in town?"

"Umm-hmm."

"What about him?"

"Well —" Her gaze fell to her lap. "Well, Turk says that Mr. Dodsworth is going to send you a letter suing you for what happened to Turk. You know, in your office here."

The phone rang. Relief replaced the fear in her eyes. She even managed to address the caller properly. "Good morning, the law offices of Sam McCain." Pause. "Oh, good morning, Mr. Hughes. Just a moment, please."

I had to clear my anger before I had enough room in my head to register surprise that William Hughes had actually called me back. I'd called him half an hour ago at the Bennett estate and left a message. I'd have to deal with Turk later. I had plenty of time to murder him. I didn't even have to buy extra bullets. I planned to strangle him. After breaking several of his more critical bones.

"Thanks for returning my call, William. I appreciate it."

"What can I do for you, Mr. McCain? The funeral's tomorrow morning, and we're all pretty busy around here."

"I just wondered how well you knew Roy Davenport."

"He was Mr. Bennett's business partner for several years. Naturally I got to know him. Why?"

"Did you ever see him with Fire Chief De-Paul?"

"Of course. Chief DePaul and Roy were out here a lot, using the tennis courts and going to parties."

"Were they friendly?"

"I'm not sure what that means, Mr. Mc-Cain. I never saw them argue, if that's what you're talking about."

"Do you think they spent time together when they weren't at the mansion?"

"Now, how would you expect me to know something like that? I didn't follow either of them around."

"DePaul and Lou were good friends, though."

"Yes. But Mr. Bennett was good friends with people he thought could do him some good. I don't say that as criticism. That's just the way business is done."

The obvious question — obvious to me, anyway — was did Bennett know DePaul well enough to ask him to lie about the origins of a fire?

Then Turk was there, and I had to force myself to concentrate on talking to William Hughes. Jamie grabbed her purse. Lunch time. She waved good-bye to me. And so did Turk. The devious prick. *Bye-bye, McCain. I'm going to be taking you for everything you've got.*

"Mr. McCain, I really am busy. There'll be a gathering here after the burial, and we need to get everything in order. I'm sure you can understand that."

"Do you recall seeing Chief DePaul out at the estate close to the date that Karen Shanlon was killed in the fire?"

He didn't answer right away. "Exactly what are you asking me?"

"I'm just wondering if DePaul was hanging around out there after the fire."

"That's an accusation, not a question. And I resent it for Mr. Bennett's sake."

"People have speculated about the fire, William."

"No, they haven't. *You* have speculated about the fire."

"Bennett didn't think she was suitable for the family."

"Not wanting her in the family is very different from wanting her dead. The man just *died,* McCain. At least give him his due and let him rest in peace."

He was gone then. He didn't slam the phone. He hung up quietly, which was his style.

Then all my anger about Turk came flooding back. Good old Turk, shiftless no-talent bum and wanna-be surfer. I'd give him the honor of drowning him in the river, which was as close to an ocean as he'd ever get.

21

She was parking her blue Schwinn bicycle as I left the office. In a Western-style red shirt and Levi cut-offs, she appeared older than she had at her stepfather's house. Or maybe it was the hair, which she'd managed to turn into a pageboy. The heavy glasses worked against all of it. She was still the lonely kid who loved *The Great Gatsby.*

"Hi, Mr. McCain."

"Hi, Nina."

"My stepfather'd kill me if he knew I was here."

"I think you're probably right about that one."

She approached me with the awkward grace of a leery animal. "I heard what you and my stepfather were talking about. He and my mother really got into it after you left. Then she found out he had a gun in the house."

"Let's talk inside. You like a Pepsi?"

"That'd be great. It's so hot."

"C'mon in. It's cooler there."

The first thing she did inside was look at my books. She passed quickly over the law tomes and went to the small bookcase where I kept novels. "We sort of have the same taste. Hemingway and Carson Mc-Cullers and Steinbeck and Fitzgerald and Malamud and Algren. But who're these writers, Jim Thompson and Charles Williams?"

"They write crime fiction."

"Is it any good?"

"Some of the best writing in America, but the critics are too snobby to review it. They think it's trash."

"Some of the covers are pretty wild." She was examining a copy of *All the Way* by Charles Williams.

"The covers are usually a lot wilder than the books themselves."

After getting her seated and pushing a Pepsi into her hand, I sat down behind my desk and got a smoke going. "You were telling me that your stepfather has a gun in the house. Doesn't he usually?"

"No. Never. My mother's little brother was killed when he found her dad's pistol and accidentally shot himself. My mother absolutely won't tolerate a gun in the house."

"Not even a hunting rifle?"

"Huh-uh. She made Ralph promise that before they got married. And my mother's never let him forget it, either."

"Did he say why he thinks he needs a gun?"

She sipped her Pepsi. Her face still gleamed from the sweaty ride over here. She wiped her forehead with the back of her hand. "He's afraid of something. I've never seen him like this. You know how he is. I'm not putting him down — not exactly, anyway. There're a lot worse stepfathers than Ralph."

"That isn't a great declaration of love."

"Oh, I don't love him. I'm not even sure my mother loves him. But most of the time he's all right. My mother's very pretty. I think that after his first wife left him, he decided to pay her back by finding the best-looking woman he could and then kind of flaunting her. My mother always laughs when she tells me about how he used to drag her to all these places just so his ex-wife would see them. But that's how he is. He usually gets his way whether my mom's comfortable with it or not. But the reason I came over here to talk to you was because after they got into this big fight about the gun she found in his suit coat pocket, I heard him say, 'Honey, I'm scared. I need to protect myself.' Boy, if you know anything about Ralph, him saying that he's scared is really something. He always acts like he's not afraid of anything or anybody. You know?"

"Did he say what he was scared of?"

"No. She asked him a bunch of times, but he said he couldn't tell her. He said it was better that she didn't know. Then he went out to the garage. That's his haven when he wants to escape. She almost never goes out there, but today she did. And they started arguing again. I was upstairs reading with the radio on, and I could still hear them."

"Could you hear what they were saying?"

"Not really. But their voices were real angry. I'm sure it was about the gun and what he'd said about being scared. I mean, if you tell somebody you're scared, shouldn't you tell them *why* you're scared?"

"You'd think so."

"My mom said that this all started this morning when Ralph heard about Roy Davenport. Ralph left the house for a while and then came back. That's when she found the gun in his pocket."

I guess the thought had been in my mind

before. But either it had been vague and fleeting, or it had been in parts that I hadn't fitted together. Lou Bennett and his enforcer Roy Davenport. If Bennett wanted to kill his son's lover in a fire, who would he have turned to? Roy Davenport, of course. I hadn't yet figured out how David Raines was involved, but his mood this morning revealed not just anger but fear.

"Is Ralph still home?"

"No. He took off before I did. My mom was so mad at him, she didn't even say good-bye. But he said it, two or three times. She wouldn't answer him. Guns really get to her."

"Will you be mad at me if I ask you why you came to my office to tell me this?"

Behind the glasses the eyes closed, and she took a deep breath. When the brown eyes opened again, she said: "I guess I sorta lied about Ralph."

"You mean about the gun?"

"Oh, no. No, I mean the part about him being okay. He's not okay. He's an a-hole. He bullies my mom and he bullies me. He even bullies our pets."

"So you came here because you thought he might be in some trouble and you wanted me to find out if it's true."

"I don't sound very nice, do I?" She

pushed the glasses back on her fine straight nose. "It's just — the other night, he hit my mom. Pretty hard, too. I saw him do it. He'd never really hit her like that before. I can't get it out of my mind."

One thing I'd gotten real tired of long ago in my law practice, men who hit women. "What night was that?"

"The night Mr. Bennett was killed."

"Did you hear him talk about Bennett dying?"

"My mother talked to him about it. We were all sitting in the living room watching TV, and during commercials she asked him about it — you know how you do when commercials come on — but he'd just sort of grunt at her or give her real short answers. My mother kept looking at me like *I wonder what's wrong with him.* Usually when something like this happens, he goes on all night. He always says we should build more prisons. He doesn't think enough people are in prison. He thinks *you* should be in prison."

I laughed. "I heard him say that FDR belonged in prison, too. I'd say that's pretty good company. How about the phone? Did you hear him talking to anybody about it on the phone?"

"No. But Roy Davenport called for him when he was gone. I got the call. This was the same afternoon."

"Did he leave a message?"

"Just that Ralph should call him back."

"Did your mother ever mention Davenport?"

"Oh, yes. He scared her. Somebody told her a couple of years ago that he carried a gun. That was all it took."

"Did she argue with Ralph about it?"

"Several times. She always said she wouldn't have him in our home, even though Ralph and he and Mr. Bennett played golf together and had poker night once a week."

"Did Ralph say where he was going when he left?"

"No. And most of the time he does. He wants her to know where he is and he wants to know where she is. That's why he calls home so often during the day. He doesn't trust her. She's still really pretty. She keeps saying that someday I'll look like her, but I doubt it." Pain in the last sentence and a frown. "They had a ninth-grade dance at the end of school this year. Nobody asked me. I asked one boy, but he turned me down. I think my mom took it harder than I did. Ralph said it was because I was quote a bookworm unquote. You know what he said?"

263

"What?"

"He actually said boys don't like girls who read books. He told me to ask the cheerleaders if any of them were big readers. He dared me to. I would've been mad, but it was so stupid. Can you see me going up to a cheerleader and asking her if she likes to read?" She had an endearing little laugh and very bright white teeth.

"You mean you didn't do it?"

"Oh, sure. That was the very first thing I did at school the next day. At lunch I sat at the cheerleaders' table and took a poll."

"Well, I'd hope so. At least you know good advice when you hear it."

"You're funny. Thanks. Now I don't feel so bad coming here. I'm just trying to get back at Ralph for bullying my mom, but I heard you asking him questions and I thought maybe I could help you."

"You've helped me a lot."

"Really?"

"Really."

She pushed up from the chair. She was a kid and a gangly one and a sweet one, and best of all she was a bookworm, reserved for boys who — despite Ralph's admonition — would cherish her for that. Among many, many other virtues.

"Our cat picked up fleas, so I have to go

to the vet to get him a new collar. He's driving the whole house crazy. We're scratching all the time. Ralph hates pets anyway. So there's another thing they can fight about."

She leaned across the desk, her hand out. We shook. "Thank you, Mr. McCain."

"My pleasure. While we were talking I wrote my home phone on the back of this card. I'd keep it in your pocket so Ralph doesn't find it."

"Oh, God, that's all I'd need, is for him to find out that I came here."

"See you later, bookworm."

She favored me with that sweet laugh again.

Roy Davenport had been killed in his garage around six A.M. He didn't usually leave the house until nine A.M. Even Cliffie wondered what had brought him out so early. He had been shot three times in the chest with a handgun. Ballistic information was forthcoming.

Pauline had slept through the shooting. She was awakened at seven o'clock or thereabouts when she heard the dog whining outside. She went to the window (my friend Molly Weaver told me this on the phone) and saw the dog standing outside the garage, whimpering. She sensed some-

265

thing wrong and grabbed her robe and hurried to the garage for a look. She found that Davenport had fallen between his car and hers. He was dead. She went in and called the police. When the cops got there, they found she'd polished off the better part of a pint bottle of Jim Beam. She was fighting her fears and her drunkenness. She had to force herself to speak past the booze so they could understand her. She demanded police protection until she could leave town, which she insisted would be before sundown. She told them she'd be going to her parents' home in Missouri. She said she'd be taking the Greyhound. Cliffie said absolutely not, that if she tried to leave she'd find herself in jail. They ended with a compromise. She'd agree to stay for three days and then she'd be free to travel. She'd reside at the Harcourt Arms hotel downtown.

The desk clerk at the Harcourt was a Shriner. I knew this because he was wearing his fez. He was also wearing sleeve garters and a bow tie. His calendar apparently ran out of pages sometime in the early 1930s. He'd been writing in a large notebook when I approached the desk. When he heard me, he looked up. Judging by the cold hard stare he gave me, I might have been Jack the Ripper.

"I have a son in the military, McCain. I just want you to know that. And the missus and I are very proud of him."

"You mean the rally the other night. If you think about it, we're on the side of your son. There's no reason to be in this war. And Johnson's going to keep expanding it and more and more of our soldiers are going to die."

He wanted to respond, but the black phone on his desk rang. He answered and started giving information about rates and availabilities. The Harcourt was second-rate, but a good second-rate. The lobby was clean and bright with solid if inexpensive couches and chairs and plants and flowers that had been well taken care of. The walls were decorated with framed black-and-white photographs of downtown Black River Falls over the years.

The three men reading newspapers and magazines weren't the old sad duffers you saw in most second-rate hotels. They were middle-aged in good clothes. They were most likely salesmen of various types.

While I waited for the desk clerk to get off the phone, two more men came in. They each toted a suitcase, they each smoked cigars, they each exuded the kind of back-slapping good will that could drive me out of a room in less than two minutes. They, too, were wearing their fezzes.

When he got off the phone, the clerk saw his two new customers. He smiled at them and said, "Just a minute, boys."

He was done arguing with me. He had work to do. "What do you need, McCain?"

I asked what room Pauline was staying in. He checked and told me and then he turned to his friends. He let me get all the way to the elevator before he started talking about me. I got whispered about a lot in this town. Sometimes I wanted to kill somebody, I got so tired of it. But where would I start, when so many people had it in for me? As the elevator reached the first floor from the fourth, I looked back at the desk. The clerk was leaning over and nodding in my direction as he spoke. The two customers were staring at me and shaking their heads. It was probably a mercy that I couldn't hear what was being said.

The narrow hall was a fault of various eras. The wallpaper and the carpeting were as dusty as ones you'd find in a hot-sheet hotel. The paintings were garish and lurid even though they were nature scenes. Probably local art. The odors were oldest of all. There were windows at either end of the hall, closed now for the air conditioning. But decades of smoking, drinking, screwing, and being sick in various ways tattooed the air forever. In the thirties, a man masquerading as a doctor had butchered a woman up here by giving her what he called an abortion. There was such outrage that a mob stormed the police station and overpowered the night officers. They got all the way back to the cells before two Highway Patrol cars pulled up. They went in with sawed-off shotguns and said they'd kill anybody who didn't leave the building immediately. Funny how persuasive a sawed-off can be.

Before I knocked, I leaned against the door. Voices. Pauline's I recognized, not the man's. I'd brought my gun. Somebody was killing people. I had no doubt they wouldn't mind adding me to the list.

The voices halted with my first knock. After a pause, Pauline said: "Who is it?"

"McCain."

The man cursed.

"I can't talk to you now. You need to come back."

"When?"

"Later."

"We need to talk now. You could be in a lot of danger."

The man's whisper was violent. Instructions.

"I'm fine. I just want to go back to sleep. You woke me up."

"You must talk in your sleep."

"What?"

"I said you must talk in your sleep. I heard you talking in there just a minute ago."

More whispered instructions.

"That was the TV. You need to come back later." She had begun pleading now.

"All right. But we really need to talk."

I walked away. I made my steps decisive. I was walking away, I was walking down the stairs, I was leaving the hotel.

I went back immediately and flattened myself against the west side of the door.

They started talking again, this time without the whispers. The male voice was familiar now. So was the word he used three times. "Letter."

This went on for ten minutes. I heard somebody coming up the stairs. I eased on over to the room next to Pauline's and bent over as if I was letting myself in. The fat salesman with the two big leather bags was out of breath. The cigarette tucked into the left corner of his mouth didn't help his breathing. He just nodded as he started to pass me. He couldn't wave with his hands full, and speaking was a bitch with a smoke dangling from your lips.

He was apparently so eager to get into his room that he didn't check back on me. He got the door open, dragged the suitcases inside and vanished.

I took up my previous position.

A few minutes later, Pauline's door opened, and I moved. I shoved him so hard and so fast that he stumbled back three or four feet before his legs folded and he landed on the floor. I kicked the door shut behind me.

"You bastard," David Raines said.

"This is getting so crazy. I don't live like this. I just want to go home and see my folks is all." Pauline's voice had risen a few octaves and was splashed with tears of hysteria. It was also sloppy with liquor. Her slurring got worse by the minute.

She wore a man's blue dress shirt that reached to the hem of her blue shorts. She had a glass of whiskey in her hand, no doubt poured from the bottle of Old Granddad on top of the bureau.

Raines got to his feet. The white golf shirt and tan slacks suggested a fun day on the links. But his eyes suggested the opposite. He couldn't decide whether to be mad or scared.

"Don't answer any of his questions, Pauline."

"I wish you'd both get out of here. I wish Cliffie would leave me alone. I wish I could get on a bus and go home. I didn't have nothing to do with any of this. Not one thing." She said all this while waggling her drink at us. I was surprised it didn't fly out of her hand, especially since her eyes had started closing every thirty seconds or so.

Raines' contempt was like an attacking animal. "You just screwed your brains out and got drunk and got fatter, isn't that right, Pauline? You didn't know about any of this. That's why you were always sneaking around when Davenport and I were talking. You knew damned well what was going on. And you wanted to cash in on it. Roy would get the final payment and then he'd take you to Europe. That was the plan, right?"

"Don't tell me no more lies, David. You're just trying to hurt my feelings since I don't know where the letter is." She was much drunker than I'd realized. She was slurring her words and putting a hand on the back of a chair for balance.

He walked over to the bureau, picked up the other glass. As he poured himself a shot, he said, "He was going to dump you. Kill you if necessary. He had it all planned out."

"I don't believe you." Which sounded like "I don' b'lief ya."

The contempt was back. "I could give a damn what you believe or don't believe. Remember the night you wanted me to go to bed with you? You think I'd let a pig like you anywhere near me?"

The alcohol seemed to protect her from the insult. She just took a deep drink from her glass and shrugged. But then she had her vengeance, as if that last drink had given her courage: "You want to know about the letter, McCain? I'll tell you about the letter."

"Shut up!" He started toward her, but I grabbed a handful of shirt and yanked him back. Before he could swing on me, I had my gun out. Her threat and the appearance of my weapon made everything much more serious.

I looked at her. I remembered the night she'd followed me in the yellow VW. She'd mentioned the letter but gave the impression she didn't know what was in it. I also remembered feeling that she hadn't told me everything. Now, with any luck, she'd tell me what she knew.

First I had to deal with Raines. "Get over there and sit down, Raines. And shut up."

"Teach you to insult me, you pig," Pauline

said. "And for your information, I wasn't trying to get you into bed. I was trying to get you to lay down before you puked all over the new carpeting the way you did that other night."

Such a lovely couple. "Tell me about the letter, Pauline. Now."

"I need a drink first." She held up her glass. It was only about a quarter full. For most people that would have been fine. For an alcoholic, it was running dangerously low. She teetered her way to the bureau, clanked herself some more of the magic elixir, and then wobbled over and sat on the edge of the emerald-green armchair. She gaped at me and said, "What was I sayin', McCain?"

"The letter."

"You're going to believe this bitch? She's so drunk, she can't even remember what she was talking about."

"Shut up, Raines. Now go ahead, Pauline."

"Did he just call me a bitch?"

"No. You just misheard him. Now tell me about the letter."

"They were blackmailing him."

I'd done enough interrogations of drunken clients to know that you had to be patient. "First tell me who 'they' are."

"They?"

"You said, 'They were blackmailing him.' "

"Hell, yes, they were."

"Tell me who 'they' are."

She jabbed her glass in the general direction of Raines. "Him and Roy."

"And who were they blackmailing?"

"You're s'posed to be a lawyer and smart'n all. Haven't you figured it out by now?"

"I think I have, but I need you to tell me."

"Lou; who else d'ya think? They was blackmailin' Lou."

"She's lying."

"Why were they blackmailing him, Pauline?"

"Why d'ya think? 'Cause he paid to have that fire set."

"Karen Shanlon?"

"Yeah, that crippled girl."

"Who did Lou pay to set it?"

She was at the stage where she had to close one eye to focus. "Him. And Roy."

"You said Raines and Roy were blackmailing him. And they set the fire, too?"

"She's drunk. Everything she's saying is a lie."

"They made him write this letter, see." She jerked backward, almost going over. I covered the distance between us in two seconds, then eased her back into the chair. She instantly poured about half the bourbon down her throat. It would be lights out very soon. Maybe that's what she was trying to do.

"You said they made him write a letter. What kind of a letter?"

She raised her head. Her eyes were gazing on a far distant world only she could see. She belched hard enough to snap her head back. Then she smiled with great grand ridiculous glory. She was working her way back to infancy.

I needed to resolve one thing for sure. I leaned down and took the drink from her hand. It took her a while to realize it was gone. "Hey, where's my drink?"

"I'll give it back to you after you answer two more questions."

"B'shish. It's *my* drink."

My face was only inches from hers. She smelled pretty bad. She looked worse.

"You said that Roy and Raines set the fire. Is that true?"

"Huh?"

I took her chin, tilted her face up to mine. "You said that Roy and Raines set the fire. Is that true?"

"Aw, shuurre. They talked 'bout it out to our house."

"And you said they were blackmailing Lou. Is that also true?"

"I wan' my drink back."

"Just answer my question and I'll give you your drink."

"Huh?"

"You said that Roy and Raines were blackmailing Lou. Is that true?"

"Yeah. They sure were. Now gimme my drink."

I gave her the drink back.

"She has to prove all this," Raines said. "You'll have a lot of luck with her on the stand. Make sure she isn't wearing a bra and that she's drunk. You'll win for sure." Raines had collected himself. He was Raines again, no longer frantic. Smug and cold now and enjoying himself.

I walked over to the phone. You didn't need a switchboard here. I dialed. Marjorie Kincaid answered. "Morning, Marj. Is Bill Tomlin there, by any chance?"

"I think so. Let me check. Hold on, Sam."

Tomlin was the uniformed cop I talked to at Lou Bennett's estate the morning he was murdered. He wasn't exactly up to FBI standards, but he wasn't stupid and he was wary enough of Cliffie's decisions to be honest.

I heard him pick up and Marjorie click off. "Can you do me a favor, Bill?"

"This is going to get me in trouble, isn't

it, McCain?"

"Yeah, but I know you've been taking those courses every summer at the police academy about how to handle investigations."

"Oh, no. The chief's moved his nephew up. He's the new lead detective. You need to talk to him."

Cliffie's nephew made Cliffie sound like Adlai Stevenson. Not an easy thing to do.

I gave him the name of the hotel and the room number. "I just want you to come over here. I want to walk you through some things. That way, at least somebody in the police department'll really know what's going on. You can leave then, and I'll call Cliffie and ask him to come over."

Raines started to get up from the couch. I'd set my gun on the small phone table. I picked it up again and this time aimed right at his head. He scowled and sat back down.

"I dunno, McCain."

"Protect and serve."

He laughed without humor. "Protecting my butt and trying to serve my family something better than Spam. That's what that means."

"That's a good one. But I'd really appreciate you coming over here. You're our only hope."

"Who's 'our'?"

"Truth, justice, and the American way."

"Isn't that from a comic book? I think it's Superman."

"I always liked Batman better."

"Yeah, me, too. Batman and the Green Hornet." He sighed. "I'll need fifteen minutes to wrap something up here."

"I really appreciate this, Bill."

By the time I hung up, Pauline was unconscious, sprawled in the chair, her drink spilled, the glass on the floor. She snored like a buzz saw.

"What a hog," Raines said. "She's disgusting. I could never figure out why Roy wanted her around."

"How much did Fire Chief DePaul get paid?"

"I'm not answering any more of your stupid questions."

I hadn't expected him to answer. I walked over to the window and looked out on the town. This high up, you could see the sides and backs of the oldest buildings, most of which bore faded business names and advertisements dating back to the 1880s and 1890s. You could see the embedded tracks of the first horse-pulled trolley. You could see the hitching posts in front of a few businesses and taverns. Time overwhelmed me sometimes, how one era appeared bright and fevered, only to dim with another new era suddenly there, bright and fevered, in this long, unending continuum. And the people walking the streets down there would be gone forever, along with their styles and songs and passions great and small, gone forever as if they never existed, even the graveyards in which they were buried disintegrating eventually. I was thinking of my dad and how he'd be gone soon and how I would ache to talk to him in the years ahead. And it would be worse for my mother. She was the one I really had to worry about.

"It won't do you any good to bring some hillbilly cop up here, McCain," Raines said to my back. "As I said, I won't be answering any questions."

I walked back to the center of the room. "That's fine. You're entitled to a lawyer. But I'll tell Cliffie everything I know, and I hope he'll take you to the station."

"He'd never go up against a Bennett."

"You're not a Bennett. And Lou's power died with him."

"What if I tell Cliffie that this hillbilly cop was up here first?"

"I'd just tell him the truth. He wasn't in when I called, so I asked for Bill."

"That's a lie. You didn't ask if Cliffie was in."

I smiled. "Well, as you said, can you prove it?"

Five minutes later, Bill Tomlin was there. Raines gave him a smirk. He looked at me and rolled his eyes. Bill's khaki uniform was a bit tight, admittedly, thanks to the weight he'd been putting on lately, but he was not stupid.

"Raines here needs to be questioned. He'll want a lawyer, but I wouldn't let him go till Cliffie has gotten answers."

"Don't call him Cliffie in front of me, okay, McCain? He was nice enough to give me a job and I'm not even a relative."

"I'm sorry, Tomlin. Pauline over there —"

"What's wrong with her?"

"Drunk and passed out."

"This room smells like a bar. So anyway, why should the chief be interested in Raines?"

"Don't believe a word this asshole says," Raines said from the couch.

"Just let him finish. Then I'll talk to you. So why should the chief be interested in him?"

"If Pauline is telling the truth, Raines and Davenport set the fire that killed Karen Shanlon. You remember that one?"

"Yeah. The wife knew her from church. She was a nice woman."

"I didn't have anything to do with it, Sergeant. He's lying, and so is that drunken whore over there."

"They apparently did it on orders from Lou Bennett. His son was still in love with Karen. Lou didn't think she was good enough to wear the Bennett nametag. And he was afraid that someday Bryce would divorce his wife and marry Karen."

"The lady in that chair over there told you all this?"

"Lady?" Raines laughed. "Are you blind, Tomlin? Look at her. She's an old bag of a slut if I've ever seen one."

"And there's a letter," I said. "Somehow it ties into the blackmail scheme they were running on Bennett."

"But weren't they all in it together? That doesn't make much sense."

"You're damned right it doesn't, Sergeant! McCain doesn't know what he's talking about."

"I don't understand it yet either, Tomlin, but somehow they ended up with Bennett paying them extortion money. That's why Raines needs to be held for questioning. There's a lot to go into."

"There sure as hell is. So, who killed

Bennett and Davenport?"

"I'd like to say Raines. But I think all we can nail him with is murdering Karen Shanlon."

"And that leaves us with who, then?"

"Somebody who plans to kill everybody who was involved in the fire. Somebody who cared about Karen enough to pay everybody back. I think Raines here is the next victim on the list."

"So that's everybody?"

"One more. DePaul."

"The fire chief?"

"Lou paid him off. Or maybe he had something on him. DePaul wrote an assessment report claiming the fire was accidental. That means he falsified a legal document."

"The chief and DePaul are good friends."

"I didn't say this would be easy, Tomlin. But I'm pretty sure you're interested in the truth. So you'll help me. You'll keep this thing on track."

"I want to call my lawyer."

"As soon as we're done here, Mr. Raines."

"Say everything you've just said is true, McCain. Or most of it, anyway. You have any idea who killed Bennett and Davenport?"

"You can't stop me from calling my lawyer."

"I have an idea, but it's not solid enough to talk about yet."

There was more. By the time we finished, Raines had slung himself horizontally on the couch and had covered his eyes with the back of his hand. When you just laid out the facts cold and hard, the case sounded pretty damned convincing, especially if Pauline could be turned into a sober and articulate witness.

"I'm sorry I had to drag you into this, Bill. If we stick to our story —"

Bill Tomlin said, "Aw, hell. Let's not try to fool the chief. I owe him my loyalty. I'll call him now and bring him over."

"Well, I did ask for him, but he wasn't in."

"That's a lie. That's a damned lie," Raines said without moving the back of his hand from his face. He sounded wasted. He'd spent his anger. He was likely thinking about life in prison.

Tomlin said, "You can call your lawyer now, Mr. Raines."

He pulled his hand back, tilted his head toward us and said, "Maybe I better call my wife first." The glamour boy had run out of glamour.

22

Lynn Shanlon's small house blazed white under the searing sun. When I pulled into the narrow drive, I saw Jimmy Adair, the next-door neighbor, just emerging from his own house with his big sloppy St. Bernard. He waved at me, then walked down his sloping front yard to the mailbox.

I knocked on the front door twice and waited for a response that didn't come. Against the faultless blue sky, a jet trail could be seen. I could hear the plane but not see it. I knocked for a third time, then decided to walk around back.

When I reached the back yard, I detoured and went over to the side of the garage. I peeked into a small dusty window. Her Dodge station wagon sat inside.

I went over to the back stoop, passing an outdoor grill as I did so. There was still a faint scent of burgers on the air. There were several blouses on the clothesline. I went over and touched two of them. Still damp. Given the heat, I knew they hadn't been hanging here all that long.

I knocked on the screen door at the back of the house. No reply. I opened the door and put my ear to the glass portion of the other door. A houseful of hums and clicks and snaps. The house robots doing their duties.

There wasn't any particular reason to be suspicious about her not being here. She might be visiting a neighbor, though she didn't seem to be the neighborly type. She might also have gone for a walk, though at ninety-three degrees it struck me as unlikely. But a friend could have picked her up and taken her somewhere.

I knocked again, waited a few minutes, then walked out front again. Jimmy Adair was down on the street with a fistful of mail, talking to an elderly bald man in scotch-plaid walking shorts and a lime-green golf shirt.

I went over and leaned against my ragtop and smoked a cigarette. The smoke was just about finished by the time Adair and the old man separated. When Adair and his St. Bernard were halfway up the slope leading to his house, I wandered over and waited for him.

"It's a son of a bitch of a day," he said, shaking his mail at me. "I wish I could handle it as well as Chauncey does."

Chauncey. I'd been trying to remember the dog's name. Chauncey came over for a pat on his massive head. I gave him three. He looked up at me with those sweet dopey eyes. He was drooling as usual, but I probably had some habits he didn't like, either.

Adair wore a red-and-white-striped shirt and jeans. He still carried himself like the jock he'd been in high school, that sense of swagger. But there wasn't any threat in him. He just clung, like many of us do, to the memories of better times. I wondered if he ever got jealous of the kids he coached at the high school, wanting the thrill and glory of being in there himself. I would have.

"I was looking for Lynn. Wondered if you'd seen her."

"Earlier I did. Around breakfast time. I was getting the paper and she was pulling out in her car. She waved and said she was going to do some early shopping. Everything all right? You seem a little tense."

"Everything's fine. I'm tense because of something that happened a little while ago. Nothing to do with Lynn."

Chauncey barked *basso profundo*. I was surprised the front window didn't shatter.

"Ol' Chauncey's hungry. It's lunchtime for both of us, I guess. The summer's going by too fast. Pretty soon I'll be eating the cafeteria food at the high school. That's one way I keep my weight down. I can't eat very much of it. I don't know what the hell they do to it, but whatever it is, the Reds could use it for torture." He grinned. "I like the gals in the cafeteria. I always feel a little guilty knocking them like that."

For me, the pitiless sun precluded any more small talk. "You know Lynn pretty well. Does she talk about Karen's fire a lot?"

He watched as Chauncey nuzzled his leg. "She was pretty mad at herself after the fire. But these days, she talks about her ex more than she talks about the fire. The three of us were all pretty good friends. It's that kind of neighborhood. I think the whole block pitched in to help her with Karen dying. But it's different with her ex. Not much we can do about that except sit and listen to her. The guy sounds like a jerk."

"Does she go out much at night?" I wanted to keep him talking. He'd started blinking a lot and licking his lips. I wanted to know what he was afraid of.

He started to speak, then stopped. He gave me one of those looks that he hoped would take him into the deep dark recesses of my mind. "What're you trying to find out here?"

"Just trying to get to know Lynn better."

"Why?"

"Thought I might ask her out."

He was silent for a time. "You didn't bother to ask if Lynn and I might be seeing each other."

"No, I didn't. And I apologize."

"Well, we're not. But you picked a strange way to ask her out. All these questions, I mean." The smile surprised me but seemed real. "Sorry if I snapped at you there. I'm very protective of her, same as I was with Karen. We all helped each other through a lot of bad times. My wife left me shortly after we moved here. I thought I would end up in a mental hospital. I lost twenty pounds in less than two months. The only thing that held me together was spending evenings with the girls here. They nursed me back to wanting to live again. And then one day I woke up and got interested in somebody else, and I couldn't believe it. I didn't care about my ex any more. That's the point I want to get Lynn to. Where she doesn't hate him any more. Because that's the grip he has on her. How much she hates him."

I put out my hand. "I appreciate all this,

Jimmy. Next time I'll be more careful about my bird-dogging."

He laughed. "Well, I hate to admit it, but I've done a little of that myself over the years. And I'm not proud of it. Ended up in bed with my best friend's girl at this drunken party one night. She blamed me for it all, and neither one of them has had anything to do with me since."

"It's a dangerous game."

"That's why all this talking we're doing makes me nervous, McCain. I had some trouble with the bottle back then, and sometimes when we talk about those days I kind of get the shakes. Lots of bad memories."

For the first time, I saw why the sisters had befriended him. There was a sadness beneath the swagger that gave him a kind of teenaged vulnerability.

"The bottle's destroyed a lot of lives. I see it every day in my line of work."

"I'm just about two years dry. I finally did something I'm proud of, besides throwing a football." Chauncey's bark rumbled across the grass. "I guess he's hungry. See you, McCain."

By the time I sat behind the wheel of my ragtop, Adair and Chauncey had disappeared into their house. I sat there, looking straight ahead at the garage, then at the house, and then back at the garage again. A momentary desolate silence ensued. Something wasn't right. Maybe she'd left town. Packed a small bag and fled. She had the best reason for killing Bennett and Davenport. Maybe she had found out about the real cause of the fire and the men behind it and had started killing them. But if she'd left town, she'd done so leaving Raines and DePaul alive. That wouldn't fit the pattern of an obsessed killer.

Her car being in the garage bothered me more than anything else. There was always the chance that she'd given in to panic and had taken a bus to the Cedar Rapids airport. Get far away before there was even a hint of anything being wrong.

But there was another person I needed to talk to as well. William Hughes had been a friend of the Shanlon family. He would also have had a good sense of just abut everything that had gone on in the mansion. What if he cared more about his relationship with the Shanlon women than his relationship with Lou Bennett? He wasn't a young man, but I had no doubt he was a capable one.

I took the ragtop out of gear and let it start to roll down the driveway. I popped the clutch and the V8 stirred into life. I had one chance of seeing Hughes. That consisted of getting to the mansion before Linda Raines learned that her husband was going to prison and would refuse to let me come inside.

I pointed my Ford eastward and set about violating some speed laws.

A middle-aged maid in a gray uniform dress and a white apron greeted me at the door. When I asked to see William Hughes she said, "I'm sorry, he's not here."

"Is he in today?"

The blue eyes showed confusion. "Well —"

"It's all right, Marilyn. I'll talk to him."

"Yes, ma'am. Thank you, ma'am." She backed out of the doorway, nodded to Linda Raines, and went back into the house.

"I'll have to get me one of those."

"I'm sure she offends your sense of justice for the poor."

"Not any more than a lot of other things."

This morning she'd gone cowgirl — a white silk blouse tucked into tailored jeans and cordovan Western boots.

Obviously Cliffie hadn't called her yet to tell her that her husband was in custody and just might not be wheeling up the old

292

driveway in his expensive sports car any time soon. If he had, Linda Raines would not be so collected and poised.

Her dark hair was gathered at the back, emphasizing the chic bones of her face. Even though the mark of beauty changed over the centuries, it was difficult to believe that her face would ever go out of style.

"You were asking about William?"

"I need to talk to him."

"You can't; he isn't here." Irritation in her words.

"You don't sound happy about that."

"To be honest, Mr. McCain, I don't understand any of this. I'm sorry I was cold a bit ago. I swing back and forth between being mad and being afraid. You caught me when I was mad."

"Have you seen William today?"

"No, and that's just it. We usually know where he is. But he wasn't here this morning. I can't even find my husband." Then: "Oh, I'm sorry. Would you like to come in and have a cup of coffee?" She wasn't faking her muddled thinking. She was going to be even more muddled and more fearful when she heard where David Raines was at the moment. But somebody else would give her that news, not me.

"No, I need to be going. I just thought I

could see William."

From her jeans she extracted a package of cigarettes. Next came a long, narrow silver lighter. After she got her cigarette going, she said, "Something was wrong yesterday. I asked him several times if there was anything I could do for him. When I was a little girl, William was my best friend and confidant. I told him everything. And every once in a while he'd tell me about himself, what he'd done with his life. He was the same with Karen Shanlon, but even more so. He spent as much time with her as he could when he was here. He was very protective of her. One of the few times I'd ever seen him stand up to my father was when Dad was telling me that Karen just wasn't right for our family. William spoke right up. He didn't attack Dad, but he made his case and didn't back down. Dad was surprised. And so was I. And that was when I realized it."

"Realized what?"

"About William being in love with Karen. I'd just assumed it was all very paternal, the way he hovered around her. But that day when he took on Dad, I heard it in his voice. He was really smitten. And I didn't blame him. Most people liked her. I think her damaged foot had given her a different perspective on life. She was good. Not phony good. But *actually* good. She was so kind and patient and loving. I liked to see her play with our cats and dogs. They took to her in ways they'd never taken to us." Then: "I feel guilty saying this, because for a long time I was a real bitch to her. I wish I could take it all back."

I remembered Wendy telling me about how rough Lou and Linda had made it for Karen. At least Linda had eventually come around.

Then I thought about what she'd just told me.

William had loved Karen. So when Karen was murdered, did William start killing the people who had taken Karen's life? Maybe I could make a case for it. The same kind of case that had Lynn Shanlon avenging her sister's death.

"Are you sure you won't come in?"

"No, thanks. I need to be going."

She angled her head so that it pointed west. "I'm going riding. It's hot, but my horse needs a good run and it'll get me out of this house. I just can't stop thinking about Dad being gone. I hated him but I loved him too. Have you ever felt anything like that, Mr. McCain?"

"All the time."

The smile was gentle. "I just hope life gets simpler the older I get."

I felt like a coward for not telling her about her husband's trouble, because her life was about to get more complicated than it had ever been.

Two minutes later, I was winding the ragtop around the circle drive in front of the mansion and heading out to see my good friend Ralph DePaul.

23

Nina DePaul was washing the family Chrysler. She'd splashed herself with the hose. Water gleamed on her thin legs. She had the radio turned to an Iowa City station that played classical music. I sure did like her, but I imagined that that book Pat Boone wrote about dating would call her taste "square." Kenny and I and our various dates had had a lot of fun passing the book around and laughing at all his bullshit advice. I strongly suspected that even now Pat was virginal. His music sure was.

"Hi, Mr. McCain."

"You must be dangerous with a hose." Her glasses were spackled with water, too.

"I just sprayed my legs to cool off. I have a lot of great ideas like that." The grin was quick and pretty.

"Is Ralph around?"

She took the soapy rag she was using and pointed to the garage. "He's been in there for about an hour. He got a phone call and then I heard my mom start crying and then he went to the garage. She's in her room. She doesn't want me to come in. I don't know what's going on. And I don't know why he's in the garage. There's nothing in there. I mean he doesn't have a little shop area like some men do. I was going to peek in, but since my mom's so upset, I don't want to make things worse by getting him mad at me."

"You say the phone call was an hour ago?"

"Maybe forty-five or fifty minutes, now that I think about it. They always rerun *Maverick* in the afternoon, and that was on when the call came."

"You like *Maverick?*"

"Yeah, but I like it better when it's James Garner and not Jack Kelly. What's so funny?"

"You. Funny and sweet." I stared down the drive to the garage. It would hold only one car. Even if DePaul had wanted a shop with a workbench and some tools, there wouldn't have been room enough for it. "There's a window on the side closest to the back yard?"

"Uh-huh. That's where I was going to peek in."

"I'll give it a try."

"Whatever it is, he was so upset he wasn't even yelling. That's the real bad sign with him. If he's not yelling. He was like that when our cocker spaniel got run over last year. We've got another TV set in the basement. He basically stayed down there alone for three or four days. My mom would take him his meals down there. I felt sorry for him. It made him seem more human to me. The funny thing was, he'd never paid much attention to Reggie when he was alive. It's like he was afraid to show how much he cared about him or something. He wants everybody to know how tough he is."

"Thanks, Nina."

A crow sat on the crest of the garage roof watching me, shiny in the sunlight. The humidity was so bad, I felt as if I was plodding through glue.

I opened the wooden gate carefully, trying to minimize the noise. I left it open. I took long cautious steps along the side of the garage until I reached the small window. I wanted to check him out before I let him know I was here. He might have hidden something in the garage — the mysterious letter came to mind — and maybe I'd get lucky and catch him with it in his hand. I realized how stupid the thought was. The heat was obviously deep-frying my brain.

He sat on a wooden stool, the heel of one shoe caught on the crossbar beneath the seat. Instead of street clothes, he wore the shirt, belt, and trousers of the Army. The leather holster at his side was empty. The .45 resided in his hand.

I always wondered if I'd get there someday. It had all gotten away from DePaul, and maybe it would someday all get away from me too. I suppose a good many of us have thought of how we'd do it if it came to that. A bullet was probably the most sensible way. Hard to miss with a bullet. The river, tall buildings, poison, I wasn't sure why, but they didn't seem right for me.

I walked to the door near the wooden gate. I knew I could get killed for my trouble but there was no way to sneak in. I opened the door. It made a scraping sound. He heard me. He slowly raised his head and studied me for a moment. I went inside.

I'd seen a number of my clients in jail suffering from clinical depression. Their responses were always lugubrious, like those of an engine that didn't want to fire. You sometimes wondered if they were awake in any real sense.

The garage smelled of heat, oil, dust, dirt. Garages had been neat places to play in my boyhood days. You could close the door and feel that you were in command of your own little world, a cowboy world or an outer space world or a Superman world.

But we were way beyond play worlds now. His despondence was as palpable and oppressive as the heat.

"Did Sykes send you? He called me."

"No. I came on my own."

"So you know?"

"Some of it, not all of it."

He raised the gun and pointed it at me. "This'd be something in the morning paper, wouldn't it? If I shot you and then took my own life?"

"Why don't you put the gun away?"

"You're scared, aren't you?"

"Sure. And you're scared, too, even *with* the gun."

He kept the gun in his hand, but he bent his head and went back to looking at the floor. His bitterness broke his gloom. "My old man screwed up at the end too. Had a good life but got hooked up with some Florida people pulling a land scam. Colonel DePaul. Perfect record until then. Died by hitting an embankment at ninety miles an hour. Everybody knew he'd done it on purpose, but nobody would say it out loud."

"What made you get involved with the fire?"

His anguished blue eyes were focused on me again. "For years I've been driving over to the Quad Cities to do a little gambling. Usually took my wife and made a weekend of it. We had some good times. And then I just got hooked. I'd drive over there two or three times a week. And it wasn't fun any more. It was serious. If I'd lose, I'd go over to win some of my money back. If I'd win, I'd go because I figured I was on a roll."

"How much have you lost?" But given what the judge had learned from the bank, I thought I already knew.

"Most of our retirement. A pretty good share of our savings."

"So your wife knows?"

"She knows about the money. She doesn't know that I let Lou pay me off." His heel came off the stool. In a single swift movement, he dropped his gun arm and jammed the .45 into his holster. "I never did have my old man's guts."

"If you cooperate, they'll go easier on you."

"Nina'll be happy. She never liked me."

"She won't be happy. She may not like you much, but she doesn't hate you. Mostly, she'll be worried about her mother."

A snort. "Her mother. I've been a piss-poor husband this time, too. Swore I'd really be different on the second go-round, and for a few years I was. But I slipped back into my old ways. My mother always called my old man a tyrant, and that's what I am too. And Nina's got every right not to like me. I wasn't much of a stepfather, either."

"You could be out in a few years."

"I'd never make it. I'd die in there."

"Not if you were careful."

His head sank again. He'd shut me out.

"Listen to me, DePaul. I need to get some things clear. Then I'll help you with Sykes. I promise."

"What a way to end up. I take a bribe and then I fink on everybody."

"They killed a woman. You're doing what you should." I paused. "You want a smoke?"

"Yeah. That'd be good. I guess I left mine inside."

I walked my pack over to him. Handed it over. He drew one out. I put my Zippo to work. In the dusty sunlight through the window in back, the smoke had a hallucinatory tumbling richness to it. I took one for myself. I needed him to give me the two names out loud.

"Who set the fire?"

"I think you've figured it out already."

"I'm asking you again, who set the fire?"

He shrugged. He'd put on some weight.

His uniform shirt revealed a small belly and a collar that was too tight. "Davenport and Raines."

"And Lou personally called you about doctoring the fire report?"

"Yeah. Lou and I were friends. It really got to me when somebody killed him. And now Davenport's dead." He dragged on his smoke. "Somebody's paying us back for Karen being killed."

"We need to stop them."

"Maybe it's better. Maybe that's what we've got coming."

"Maybe so. But that's not for you to decide. That's what we've got courts for. And by the way, Lynn Shanlon seems to be missing."

He eased off the stool. I took two steps back. He still had a gun, and he still had a reason to try and escape. "I was thinking she was the one who killed the two of them. She has the biggest stake in all this. If Karen had been my own sister, I'd go after everybody involved."

"I need to take you in now."

"I figured."

"The first thing is, you have to hand your .45 over to me."

He touched the holster. "I've had this since Korea. Killed two Chinks with it on the same day. My old man always told me how good it felt to kill somebody. But he was a bullshitter. At least *I* didn't feel good about it. I didn't feel anything. I was just doing my job. I didn't even talk about it with my soldiers. When they killed somebody, you never heard the end of it. But I was quite a bit older than they were. Maybe it would've felt good to me if I'd been their age."

All the time he talked I watched his gun hand. Maybe he was using his words to snake charm me into carelessness. I start watching him instead of watching his gun hand. . . .

He did it in the same kind of swift motion as when he'd pointed it at me. He handed it over without any kind of ceremony. He just laid it across my open palm.

"I'd like to talk to my wife."

"Fine."

We didn't talk now. He went first out the garage door and into the staggering heat. The back of my shirt was swimming-hole wet and my armpits were heavy with water. He walked to the back door. He didn't look back. He went inside.

I walked up to where Nina was still working on the car. She was hunched down, scrubbing the front left tire. She dipped a

305

wiry brush into a soapy bucket of water.

"You find him, Mr. McCain?"

"Yeah."

"He talk to you?"

"Uh-huh."

"He in trouble?"

"The Grand Inquisitor."

She grinned. "Dostoyevsky. I read that last year. *The Brothers Karamazov* is one of my favorite novels."

She stood up. Bones making a cracking sound. "I must be getting old." The grin again.

Then we heard the scream.

"My mom," she said and flung her brush into the soapy water of the bucket. "I need to see what's wrong."

Her mother had been told the truth; that was the problem. Her husband would most likely be going to prison. The family would be disgraced. And what about finances? Mrs. DePaul had to be thinking about that, too, with Nina soon to be starting college.

Nina ran alongside the house, half-crashed through the backyard gate, and disappeared. There was no other scream, but there was plenty of sobbing. Mrs. DePaul sounded as if she was on the verge of insanity. The wailing was stark and inappropriate in this expensive housing development. This was the kind of wailing you heard in Negro ghettos and in poor white neighborhoods, where mothers worn down by years of terrible news about mates and children reached some kind of end game and broke down entirely, unable to handle even one more call from the police or crawl their way one more time to identify one more body in the morgue.

In the midst of the wailing, DePaul appeared in the backyard gate. He closed it behind him just before he started walking toward me. He'd changed clothes. In his white shirt and blue trousers and tasseled black loafers he walked with the military stride I'd seen so often. Some of his self-confidence was back.

"My attorney says I should drive myself to the police station and not talk to you at all any more."

"I'm an officer of the court, DePaul. If you don't want to talk to me, that's fine. Your lawyer's right. But I want to deliver you personally to the police station."

"You must want your picture in the paper." It might have been a joke, but I knew better. His wife whooped again. He cringed. His eyes roved to the house. "I wish she was tougher."

"I'm assuming you told her."

He looked at me again. "That's what I get for telling her the truth, I guess. All through the years, I've kept bad news away from her as much as I could. She just goes all to hell. She's a nervous type anyway." He took his cigarettes from his shirt pocket. "You're not thinking of handcuffing me or anything, are you? Because if you are, you're going to find yourself in a fight."

"That'd probably cheer your wife up, seeing you and me trying to punch each other out."

"Goddammit, McCain, at least let me have a *little* dignity. I don't want people in town to see me in handcuffs."

The wailing was loud again now. It had that lonely sound of wolves on winter nights.

"You're getting worked up for nothing, DePaul. You brought up handcuffs, I didn't. I don't even *have* any handcuffs." He was letting paranoia take him. He was worried about his dignity. Even in a small city jail like Cliffie's, the cell would take his dignity away in a way he'd never experienced before.

"C'mon, McCain. Let's get out of here before Nina comes back. I couldn't face her now. Later — but not now."

I'd just backed to the end of the driveway when Nina opened the front door and

308

watched us leave. She didn't wave or call out. She just watched. Once we were in the street and ready to head downtown, I waved to her. She didn't wave back. DePaul kept his head down, pretending not to see her.

"You can look up now, DePaul. We're a block past your house."

"My wife'll hate me the rest of her life."

"Maybe not. You can't judge her right after you've told her what you've done. Even if you didn't mention going to prison, she can figure it out for herself."

"The same with Nina, Nina'll probably hate me the rest of her life too."

He just might have been right in that particular judgment. Nina just might hate him all her life. She just well might.

24

Clifford Sykes, Jr. sat on the edge of his desk as I told him everything I knew about David Raines and Ralph DePaul. I detected a certain pleasure in his eyes when I was talking about Raines. Raines had never made his contempt for "the hillbilly" a secret. But the pleasure became sadness when I told him about his friend DePaul. His jaw muscle worked and he smoked in a chain.

We'd been at it for half an hour. He'd told Marjorie he wouldn't be taking any calls, and he yelled at anybody foolish enough to knock on his door.

"Lou and Ralph. They were my friends."

He slid off the desk and rubbed his butt. Apparently it had gone to sleep. Then he walked behind his desk and sat down. The news had shocked him into humility. He hadn't yet called me a shithead or an asswipe, two of his more recent names for me. But then I hadn't insulted him either.

"Lou helped build this town. He employed a hell of a lot of people and he was always behind making things better. He had that foundation and it donated a lot of money. Hell, Lou built that swimming pool for those colored kids just last year." He was talking to himself. He was still trying to convince himself that this was real. "And poor Ralph's wife. She's real high-strung and she's had a lot of health problems. This sure won't be good for her. This is the kind of thing that can kill people." I remembered her scream as I stood on the DePaul drive earlier. The terrible grief of it. "Him and that damned gambling. I warned him about it. He used to sneak off to the Quad Cities. Friend of mine spotted him over there several times. I brought it up to Ralph, and he promised me he wouldn't do it any more. He lied. And he just got in deeper."

He leaned back in his chair. He chewed on the inside of his cheek, and then he said: "If all this is true, McCain — and it probably is — that still leaves us with two murders." Despite the air conditioning, his tan khaki shirt was spotted with sweat. "Somebody who wanted to pay them back for being involved in that fire."

"That's how I read it."

"You got any ideas?"

I swallowed a smile. I imagined Judge Whitney's face when I told her that he'd actually asked my opinion. The old judge would have ordered up a bottle of the best. The new judge would just sip her ginger ale.

I lied, because I felt as if I'd done all the work so far and I wanted to finish it off myself. "Not really. Just possibilities."

"What kind of possibilities?"

"Just ideas that I still need to think through."

The way he looked at me, I knew he would soon be calling me names again. "You're hiding something."

"I'm really not, Chief. I just need time to think my ideas through."

"That's the trouble with you, McCain. All talk and no action."

Let's see, I'd brought him Raines and De-Paul while he'd brought nobody. Most of the time I would have defended myself, but now all I wanted was to leave. "I'm just try-ing to take my time with things."

"What'll they do to Ralph?"

"If he cooperates right now, that'll help. Hell, Chief, your cousin's the district at-torney. You can put in a good word for Ralph."

"Yeah, he's my cousin all right, but we

had this family reunion out to the park last weekend and I guess I kind of called him a cheat. You know, at cards? I had a few too many beers, I'll admit that, and he was whopping me every hand, so I shot my mouth off. My wife, she made me call him the next day and apologize. The jerk."

"He wouldn't accept your apology?"

"He called me a clown."

"That's too bad."

" 'Clown' is worse than 'cheat,' isn't it?" But he didn't wait for an answer. "I guess I can always ask my dad to talk to him about Ralph. He's scared of Dad just like everybody else."

He was so damned dopey, I sort of liked him for a fleeting moment. I used his funk to say, "I need to be going, Chief."

He waved me off. "I suppose Raines'll bring in some hotshot from Chicago for his lawyer."

"Probably."

And then he brought me back to reality. He smiled like a plump idiot baby and said, "Nobody'd want some dipshit lawyer like you, that's for sure."

All the way down the hall, as I headed for the front door, I could hear him laughing.

As soon as I opened the outer door to my

office, I heard their voices. Jamie and Wendy. I got myself a Pepsi from the machine I shared with the store up front and then strolled into my office. I say strolled because the heat had started to slow me down considerably. I didn't mind the moisture in my shorts all that much, but the sweat on the bottoms of my feet bothered me. I felt as if I was walking on sponges.

I walked over and kissed Wendy on the top of her head; then I went to my desk, dropped into my chair, and let the rumbling window air conditioner work its noisy miracle. I rolled the Pepsi bottle back and forth over my forehead.

"You look tired, Mr. C."

All I could manage was a grunt in response.

"Jamie and I were just saying you work too hard."

Another grunt.

"That's why I stopped in, Sam. How about grilling some shrimp and eating some potato salad I made? That's my specialty. Then a relaxing evening on my veranda, where it's cool as soon as the sun starts to go down."

"He'll never be able to say no to that, Mrs. Bennett."

"Oh, you never know about Sam, Jamie.

He might tell me that he's too busy."

"But Mr. C needs some time off and this sounds really good."

"You and I know it sounds good, but does *he* know it sounds good?" Wendy looked like a coed in a light-blue blouse, dark-blue culottes, and white tennis shoes.

"I wouldn't miss it. Thank you very much for the invitation."

"See," Jamie said. "I told you."

An odd smile broke wide on Wendy's face. "Tell him your news, Jamie."

"What news?" The artificial air was beginning to chase the sweat from me.

"You know when I asked you for an advance?"

"Uh-huh."

"Well, I started thinking about what you said. And then I started thinking about all the money I've already given Turk, Mr. C. And you know what I came up with?"

"No. What?"

"I decided to tell him that I wouldn't loan him any more money because I was broke myself, always borrowing ahead and everything. And even when he started yelling at me, I didn't change my mind. I did it just the way Mrs. Bennett told me to."

"Wendy told you to do it?"

"Yes, Mr. C. We just started talking while

315

we were waiting for you, and I was telling her about Turk and everything, and she said that if he really loved me, he'd get a job and not keep asking me for money. A surfer band from Iowa kind've confused her, too, I think. Anyway, she told me just what to say and that's what I did." She smiled at Wendy. "It was kind of funny, she was coaching me while I was talking. I had a hard time not laughing."

"I'm very proud of both of you."

"And, oh yeah, William Hughes called. He said he'd call you back."

"Didn't say what he wanted, though?"

"Huh-uh. He said he was in Cedar Rapids and would call when he got back."

I sat up straight, set the Pepsi bottle on the desk and said, "How long ago did he call?"

"About two hours ago, I guess."

Two hours would have given him plenty of time to drive back from Cedar Rapids. I reached in the drawer and retrieved the phone book. Lou Bennett wasn't listed. But then why would he be? All rich men in small cities are, fairly or unfairly, resented by a share of the populace. Having your number listed would be asking for nuisance calls of all kinds.

Then I realized that the heat really had

slowed my thought process. Sitting across from me, and looking quite plucky for all the heat, was Linda Raines's sister-in-law.

"I'm assuming you know the number of the Bennett estate?"

"Sure."

I wrote it down as she gave it to me, and then I picked up the receiver and dialed.

The voice I heard on the other end was strained, tight. "This is the Bennett residence."

"Who's speaking, please?"

"This is the maid."

"This is Sam McCain. Is Linda there?"

There was a long pause. "She can't come to the phone right now. I'm sorry, Mr. McCain."

"Then how about William Hughes? Is he around?"

Even though I didn't hear another voice, I pictured somebody coaching her, the way Wendy had coached Jamie. "I'm afraid he's busy, too." She paused, and then like an actor who'd suddenly remembered her line she said: "They're working on plans for the funeral."

"I see."

The temptation was to ask if everything was all right, but obviously it wasn't all right; and if I asked it, I'd only be putting her in more difficulty. "Would you please ask one of them to call me at my office?"

"Yes, of course. Good-bye now."

"Don't you want my number?"

This time I did hear another voice. An angry director not happy with how his in-génue was performing.

"Oh, yes, Mr. McCain. I'm sorry. Of course I want your number. What is it, please?"

I gave it to her, but I doubted she wrote it down.

"Please have them call me. It's important."

"I will. Good-bye, Mr. McCain."

After I hung up, I sat there sorting through everything I'd just heard. Something was wrong out at the Bennetts'. Maybe it was just an angry family argument. Maybe Linda and Hughes were going at each other. That's not uncommon following a death. Old grudges are aired and bitterness thrives. I had a client once who wanted me to sue her sister for belting her in the eye. They'd argued over who had really been their dead daddy's favorite. I finally talked her out of the suit but lost her as a client.

"What's wrong, Sam?"

"I'm not sure. The maid sounded as if there was some kind of trouble there. I think somebody was telling her what to say."

"Linda's probably hysterical with David in jail. She can be hell on wheels when she's upset."

"I like that," Jamie said, "hell on wheels."

"By the way, Sam, hell on wheels reminds me. Tomorrow night Cartwright is going to try again. He couldn't get all those Beatles records burned, so now he's going to stand on that little bluff out at the lake and throw them into the river."

I wished I had time to enjoy the image of Cartwright firing the Satan-spawned records into the dark waters, but that would have to wait. The Pepsi and the air conditioning had helped revive me, but not enough for the trip I needed to make now.

"I need to go down the hall." Jamie knew what I meant. She always said "little girls' room," so I decided to euphemize my own duties.

Wendy looked confused.

"He means the little boys' room," Jamie said.

"Thank you, Jamie."

"You're welcome, Mr. C."

Wendy found this amusing. She looked even better when she was laughing.

In the john, I took off my shirt and proceeded to the tiny sink. I ran cold water, grabbed three paper towels, and started washing my upper body. Then I stuck my head under the faucet and began scooping cold water on my head. Two doors down, I could get a cup of atomic coffee. It didn't taste very good, but one cup could keep you awake for as long as a month.

I combed my hair, leaving it wet. I reached across to the peg where I kept an extra shirt. This was a short-sleeved blue JCPenney button-down.

When I walked back into my office, Jamie was on the phone. It was a Turk call. She had that look. There was a Turk call expression for happy and a Turk call expression for sad and a Turk call expression for mad. This one was sad. "I told you, Turk. I still love you, but I just can't give you any more money. You need to get a job. And I shouldn't be wasting Mr. C's time by talking about this at the office. Now I need to go."

After she hung up, she breathed deeply, made fists of her small hands, and said, "Was that all right, Mrs. Bennett?"

"Perfect. And will you please call me Wendy? You're driving me nuts with that 'Mrs. Bennett' business. I feel old enough already."

"Well, you're not that old. I'll bet you're not even forty yet."

Now it was my turn to be amused. Wendy was six months younger than I was, which meant she was twenty-eight. Jamie had no concept of peoples' ages. She once guessed my age and put it at forty-six.

"I'm actually forty-three, Jamie."

"You are? Well, you've held up very well. Wouldn't you say so, Mr. C?"

"Remarkably well."

Then I needed to fortify myself. I have a drawer gun and a glove compartment gun. I decided on the Smith & Wesson .38 I keep in the office. I can hide it better in my clothes. "Now I have to leave."

"Am I supposed to pretend I didn't see you shove a gun in your back pocket?" Wendy did not sound happy.

"You did. And it's nothing to worry about. Just a precaution."

"Don't worry," Jamie said. "He takes guns out a lot of the time. He knows what he's doing."

Wendy's mouth was tight, her gaze disapproving. "I'm not much for guns, Sam."

"You know what?" Now I sounded a bit irritated myself. "Neither am I. Now c'mon, I'll walk out with you."

Before leaving, Wendy walked over to Jamie and took one of her hands and said, "I gave you my phone number. You call me whenever you want to talk. This won't be easy for you, Jamie. But you've got to do it."

"I know you're right — Wendy. It's just so hard when I think about all the fun we've —" She was starting to cry.

Wendy kissed her on the cheek. "You're a lot stronger than you think you are, Jamie. And remember to call me when you need some moral support."

Tears gleaming in her eyes, Jamie nodded, then turned away from us so she could cry in private.

Outside, as we walked to our respective cars, Wendy said, "She's so pretty and so sweet."

"Even though she thinks you're forty?"

"I didn't say she was brilliant. But I like her. She's kind of down-home folks."

"Thanks for helping her. I've been trying for years to get her to stand up for herself — you managed to do it the first time out."

"He was just taking such advantage of her."

We were at her shiny black Chevrolet Impala. She poked me in the stomach. "I take it you're going out to Lou's place."

"Uh-huh. Something's wrong."

"Marilyn's almost always very pleasant. They had to go through a number of maids before they found her."

"You're making my point. She didn't sound pleasant at all. She sounded scared."

"I wonder if William's there. He wouldn't let anything happen."

"The maid said he was, but I don't know if that's the truth."

She touched my arm. "I hate to say this, but why not call Cliffie and let him take care of it?"

I kissed her gently on the mouth. "I don't blame you for hating to say that. I'd be ashamed to say it."

Another poke in the stomach. "My he-man. And not a brain in his head."

She slid her arm around me, two sweaty, lonely, even desperate people. When I was with her, I felt good, safe in some way. She told me she felt the same way. We both agreed this didn't mean we'd be going out all the time. But then we both agreed that it didn't not mean we'd be going out all the time, either. I guess if you wait long enough, those cheerleaders come through for you after all. Last night we'd gone all the way to third base; and lying there afterward, sharing a cigarette, I realized how much I just plain liked her. The pain of her divorce and loneliness had changed her. She was no longer the belle of the ball, because the ball had ended; the fiddlers had fled.

She walked me over to my car and saw me safely seated. "You think you'll ever give this convertible up?"

"Please. Not 'convertible.' Ragtop."

"Oh, I see, just like in all those Henry Gregor Felsen novels my brother used to read. My brother always wanted to have my father drive him to Des Moines to meet him." Felsen wrote teen novels for boys. Most of them involved cool cars. They were among the most popular books in American libraries.

I started the car. "I wanted to do the same thing. Maybe I still will someday."

I backed out, beeped the horn when I'd gotten the car turned around.

She waved good-bye and damn, that felt good. I gave her a little Lone Ranger wave of my own and sped off.

25

Dark clouds had started moving in from the west. Though the day was dying, the heat had not relented. Lawns without sprinklers looked naked. Hoses were still the preferred choice of fun for giggling kids. Women wore straw hats with brims as wide as an eagle's wingspread. Old couples sat on old porches, intimate in their silence.

Traffic was slow because factories and businesses and shops had just closed. When I got on the secondary road leading to the Bennett place, I added twenty miles an hour to the speed limit.

When I was near the estate, I pulled over to the side of the road and cut the engine. I wanted to find out if something was wrong in the house. Announcing myself was not the way to do it.

Adjacent to the estate was a forest of pine and oak. The estate had no fence around it. It would be possible to work my way parallel to the back of the house through the trees and then run for the house without being seen. Possible, but no guarantees.

The trail I found was so narrow that I had to fight low-hanging branches all the way. Any good the sponge bath had done me was quickly lost. I streamed with sweat, both from walking and swatting at any number of flying things that seemed to find me tasty. I tripped once over an extended tree root and was dropped to my knees. Amazing that you can feel humiliated even when you're alone. I was really pissed at that tree.

All the time I walked, I could see the estate house as a dim form broken by various tree parts. At the point where I planned to sneak across to the back door, I left the pitiful trail and battled my way through branches that were ready for the contest. By the time I reached the edge of the woods, I had cuts on my forehead, my cheek, and my throat. Something had ripped into my right sleeve and cut a hole in it. Sweat had filled the bottoms of my shoes again. Comedians called it flop sweat, but I didn't like the implications of "flop."

I crouched beneath a pine tree and gazed out past the heavy shadows to the estate grounds. I checked every window facing me. Empty. The rear of the place was static; it could have been a still photograph. The three-stall garage, the barn, the stable, and the black car William Hughes drove stood in the fading sunlight, their colors dimming now in the lingering plunge into dusk.

I took my handkerchief from my back pocket and tried to wipe myself dry, at least dry enough to hold off any more irritation about the weather. I needed to think clearly and act quickly. Without sweat in my eyes, I scanned the rear of the estate again and decided to make my move.

The run was simple. No problem at all. I stood at the back door, my hand on the knob. I checked the back yard in case somebody was watching from one of the buildings; but seeing nobody, I turned the knob. The door wasn't locked.

I took a deep breath and eased my way inside. I closed the door behind me with exaggerated care, a pantomime of caution. Stairs led straight down to the basement. On my left were two steps. These led to another closed door that would open on, most likely, the kitchen area. I took the first one and leaned my head against the door. All I could hear was the chatter of the house itself. The plumbing was particularly noisy at the moment. No human noise.

I took the second step, turned the knob.

Only then did I become aware of the air conditioning. My impulse was to just stand there and appreciate it.

The kitchen would have served a big-city hotel very well. Two large stoves, a wall of small appliances, a refrigerator that could hold a water buffalo, and a butcher block table running down the center of it all that resembled the deck of an aircraft carrier. Lou had taken his food very seriously.

A red sun was creeping down the window by the sink. A haze was settling across the land. In all those Hammer movies I saw at the drive-in, this is when we saw Dracula's eyes come open in his coffin. My eyes were wide open now, too, because somewhere in the house somebody was speaking.

I pulled the .38 from my belt. I moved forward one quiet step at a time, drawn by the voice. All I could tell from here was that a male was speaking.

The kitchen led me to a hallway that stretched from front to back of the place. Near the vestibule I could see the bottom of a staircase that curved out slightly. The voice was coming from a room in that area.

Getting in had been easy enough. This was where it became real work. I didn't like the exposure that being in the hallway forced on me. If somebody peeked out of that room, I'd have no place to hide. I started walking on tiptoe.

When I got close enough to make sense of the words being spoken, I stopped and listened.

"You weren't her friends. You said you were. But you lied. I was the only real friend she had. I tried to let it go. I took long trips to try and forget about it. I wanted to get on with my life, but I couldn't. Then when her birthday came this year —

"I took care of Bennett and Davenport. I would've taken care of Raines, too, but the law got to him first." Then: "You're going to open that safe for me and you're going to do it right now."

I still couldn't identify him. The voice was familiar, but I couldn't put a name or a face to it. Not anybody I knew well.

A closet door on my right was open a few inches. Glancing inside, I saw her slumped against the wall. The gray maid's uniform was distinctive.

I jammed the .38 back down into my belt-line and then tended to her as best I could.

This was used as a storage closet. Boxes lined the opposing walls. The center where she lay was open.

I knelt down next to her. When I touched her wrist, her eyes opened. I put a finger to my lips and shook my head. Recognition showed in the blue eyes. The smells were a mixture of perfume, talcum powder, and blood. Her pulse was stronger than I'd expected. She started to sit up, but her body spasmed with pain. She started to fall back against the wall, but I grabbed her before she hit. She didn't need any more pain, and neither of us needed any noise. I still didn't know who was ranting on in the living room.

She exhaled in a shaky burst, then began searching her skull with trained careful fingers. She found the wound. When she took her fingers away, they were stained with blood. She examined them without any emotion I could see, like a nurse assessing a patient's injury. She scowled then. Anger. Good. Right now, that was the most appropriate emotion of all.

We reverted to pantomime. I jabbed my finger in the direction of the kitchen. She gave a slight nod. Even that caused her to wince. I pantomimed standing up. She gave me a shrug. Maybe, maybe not. I got to my feet and then reached down and took her hand. The flesh was callussed and very cold. We started her long, painful trip upward. She rose by a few inches at a time. When she was halfway up, she started to slump against the wall. I got my arm around her waist to steady her and kept it there for the rest of the journey. She was a thin woman of maybe fifty. I'd made the mistake of thinking she was frail. But as she rose, I could feel her strength pushing against the damage that had been done to her head and her senses. There were a lot of prairie people like her. They'd brought their strength out here from the East. Without that kind of backbone, they would never have survived the daily perils of the frontier.

I let her lean against me as we shuffled into the hallway. The man in the living room was still ranting. And ranting it was, a fuming harangue about how they'd betrayed Karen. The words filled the hall. I thought of the Boris Karloff picture *Bedlam* and how the asylum inmates screamed threats and curses as they flung themselves against the bars of their cages.

We had to stop halfway to the kitchen because she thought she was going to be sick. But she raised her head and opened her mouth, taking in gulps of air. She clutched my arm as she did this. The tough grasp got even tougher for a moment. Then she exhaled and took a step forward. We moved slowly on to the kitchen.

I got her seated in the breakfast nook and went to get her a glass of water. As she took her first sips, I yanked the .38 from my belt. She'd been looking at it. I spoke in a voice a bit higher than a whisper.

"What happened?"

She set the glass down and wiped her mouth with her fingers, leaving a ghost of blood on her lower lip. "Mrs. Raines and William and Lynn Shanlon were in the living room talking about everything that had happened lately. They were wondering who killed Mr. Bennett and Roy Davenport. Lynn said all this had to have something to do with her sister's murder. That's what she called it this time. Murder. Somebody rang the front bell, and I opened the door and it was a man with a gun. He was standing right next to me when you called. He kept pushing the gun into my back. Then he knocked me out and put me in the closet."

"Do you know him?"

"No. I'd never seen him before. But he looked — insane. Very crazy. His face. Even without his gun, he would have scared me."

"So he's got all three of them in the living room?"

Her answer was to grab the edge of the table for support. Her face had gone pale and her blue eyes had dimmed. I'd estimated her age at fifty. Right now she looked seventy.

"I think I need to see a doctor."

"I think you're right." I was up and getting her more water. She'd drained the first glass. "Is there any whiskey around in the kitchen?"

"That's all right. I can't stand the stuff anyway." She rested her head against the back of the nook. She closed her eyes. I brought her water to her. Her breathing came in torrents.

I didn't sit down again. "I'm going to see what I can do in the living room. I'd call the police but I don't know what he'd do if he heard a siren."

"He's insane, I know that much. I told you about his eyes."

Put my hand on her shoulder. "You just rest."

She patted my hand. She still hadn't opened her eyes. "You be careful."

The lunacy in his voice was compelling. He was like a deranged Pied Piper. By the time I reached midpoint in the hallway, I realized what he wanted. If he had all the money in Lou's safe, he would be able to flee. And he would let them live. Well, that was bullshit, and I knew they knew that was bullshit. As soon as he got his money, they'd all be dead.

Linda's voice was calm. "I've told you,

Jimmy, I don't have the combination. You don't know anything about my father if you think he'd trust anybody with it."

"Then the colored fellow here, he knows it."

William Hughes's voice was steady, too. "We've been over and over this, Mr. Adair. Mr. Bennett would never give that combination to anybody. And I mean *anybody*. He wasn't what you'd call trusting."

Jimmy Adair, Lynn's next-door neighbor.

"You wouldn't even help your own sister, Lynn. You would've let them get by with it. That's why I had to step in."

He was jumping subjects. When he spoke to Lynn, his voice went up an octave and the madness was clearer.

Lynn wasn't as calm as Linda or Hughes. She sounded as if she was ready to snap. "You killed two people, Jimmy. You think that's what Karen would have done? You killed two people for nothing. It didn't bring her back, did it? And now you're going to kill us. You need help, Jimmy. Even if you had money, you're in no condition to get away. You're — upset. You're not thinking clearly." Then, "William and I spent most of the day talking to a fire investigator in Cedar Rapids. We wanted him to go over the whole report again, see if we could get the investigation reopened. William and I never believed that fire was accidental. That's what Karen would have wanted us to do — not kill people."

"I killed the people who killed her — why is that so hard to understand?" His voice cracked; tears rattled his words. "I loved her. If she'd lived, I would've asked her to marry me. And she would have, too." He turned to Linda. "Your father took away the one woman I ever really loved, so I figure he owes me — that's why I want every dollar in the safe. Every single dollar. Then I'm leaving this town and never coming back."

They didn't dare argue with him. Not when he was in the midst of his frenzied fantasy.

The gun blast was so loud, I felt it as well as heard it. And almost directly on top of the blast, I heard a grunt and then the sound of something heavy hitting the floor. And on top of that came Lynn's shriek and Linda's sob. Linda cried: "You killed him! You killed him!"

"He shouldn't have thrown that ashtray at me. He was stupid."

Hughes, a military man, had waited for what he considered his best opportunity. He'd taken the calculated risk of trying to injure or at least distract Adair. Then he would rush in and tackle him. It had been a long, long shot. But it was preferable to just sitting there listening to the madman as he worked himself into the kind of rage it would take to slaughter three people.

In the confusion of screams and shrieks, I was able to run the rest of the way down the hall without being heard. Adair was shouting at the two women to sit back down, sit back down. There were tears in his words; he was coming undone. He might turn on the women at any point.

Lynn saw me before he did. In fact, it was her recognition that made him spin toward me and fire twice. The second shot ripped into my shoulder and jerked me backward two or three feet. I fired my .38, but the shock of being wounded marred my aim. My own two shots ripped into the wall behind him. Glass shattered.

Lynn was on him now, fighting for his gun. She slapped at him and shoved him and got her hand on his gun wrist.

I started to move, the pain in my shoulder exploding now. This time, the sweat covering me was cold. I managed to get within six or seven feet of him, but that was when he slipped his arm around her throat and swung her around to face me. He'd managed to get himself a hostage.

From where I stood now, I could see William Hughes flat down on the surface of a Persian rug. Linda Raines was crouched next to him, tears glazing her cheeks.

The pain from my wound ran the length of my gun arm. I was having trouble holding the .38. Bad enough he had Lynn. It would be even worse if he had Lynn and I dropped my gun.

"You listening to me, Lynn?" He increased his grip on her throat. She made a choking sound, her upper body surging instinctively as her breathing was cut off. "We're going outside and getting in your car. And we're going to drive out of here. Do you understand me?"

I called on all the private-eye writers I read. I needed their encouragement and guidance. They were always getting clubbed, stomped, stabbed, burned, drowned, and shot, but nothing stopped them from their appointed vengeance. Sure, they had six shots in their chest and one in their head, but by God they always managed to get the job done.

I was falling a little short of their record of accomplishments. All I had was a wound in my shoulder, and here I was dizzy, cold, and losing strength. I was afraid I was going to pass out. I wasn't going to get a private-

337

eye merit badge for this one.

I had a gun, but Adair had Lynn. "You could've helped, too, McCain. People always say you help when they're in trouble. You should have figured out that that fire was arson. You owed it to Karen."

"I didn't know Karen."

"Everybody knew Karen, and everybody loved her, too."

Any other time, his madness would have made him a forlorn figure living out some impossible romance in his mind. But he had the gun and he had Lynn and he had already killed two and maybe three times, depending on how William Hughes was. Pity him afterward, Samuel Johnson had said of hanging killers in old London. That applied here too.

He began moving in small jerky steps toward the hall. He wasn't having an easy time of it. Shuffling along with a hostage in tow isn't easy. You have to keep a tight grip on her while always keeping track of what the other guy is doing. The hostage could make a break for it; the other guy could make a sudden move you couldn't respond to quickly enough.

Then I realized his plan. He wasn't going to take her with him. He was going to use her to get to the car and kill her before he got in it. Nobody was guiltier than Lynn, by his logic. Karen had been her sister. She'd betrayed Karen by not avenging her death. He'd killed the men involved. Now he would have to kill her too.

"God, stop him, Sam! Stop him!" Lynn's voice was raw, her face a portrait of confusion and shock. Spittle ran down the left side of her mouth. Her knees kept buckling. Adair had to redouble his grip every thirty seconds; otherwise, she'd slide out of his grasp. She slipped into the low moan I'd heard many times in people who were starting to withdraw from reality following a traumatic event. She was coming apart. I had to help her.

I forced myself to stand up straight. For the moment, Adair was wrestling with her to keep her upright. She had to cooperate. If he had to drag her, he'd leave himself open. I'd get an easy shot at him.

I took two steps and started weaving. A new layer of freezing sweat caused me to shiver. Just moments ago I'd been boiling despite the air conditioning.

As I righted myself, my eyes met Adair's. He had Lynn back under his control. He was watching me closely. I assumed that to him, I might have been trying to distract him, give Lynn a chance to bolt. He couldn't be sure whether I was for real or just acting.

"God, McCain, are you all right?" Lynn said.

"Doesn't look like your savior's going to save you." Adair vised her neck even tighter.

The worst of the cold was gone, one large convulsion of it that had nearly knocked me down. My palm was so sweaty, I had to squeeze the gun so tight that it hurt. I was still dizzy. I needed to move with great deliberation.

Adair started moving again. They went three or four steps and she kicked him. Both his face and his voice registered the pain. For a millisecond his grip loosened, just enough time to take a single unencumbered step. But he was quick and he was pissed. He swung her back to him and smashed the side of her head with the bottom of his gun. She slumped in his arm. Blood snaked down from her temple. He was better coordinated than I'd guessed. His eyes had never left me.

But he paid a price for knocking her out, and as he started moving again, he discovered what the cost was. Conscious, she walked with him. Unconscious, she was dead weight. An ungainly hundred-pound bag of flesh, bone, blood, and water. He cursed. He couldn't just hold her now, he had to hold her and drag her.

Another convulsion rocked me. I needed to reach out for something to lean against, but there was nothing. A drunkard's walk as I tried to move forward. One step, two steps, three —

This time I couldn't stop myself from starting to fall. I didn't sprawl, though. I was able to hold my descent to one knee.

And that was when it happened. I wasn't sure of anything until it was over. Instinct guided me. I was too weak to think anything through.

When I dropped to my knee, he opened fire. But he hadn't been fast enough to follow me down. Two blasts went over my head and tore into some kind of glass in the living room.

He got so intent on killing me that he loosened the arm that held Lynn. She slipped from his grasp to the floor, leaving him unprotected.

I fell sideways because of sheer weakness. He blasted at me again but again he wasn't quick enough. He'd fired just as I slumped over.

I had a target and I took it. Somehow before it all came crashing down, I got a shot off. I was conscious long enough to see him start to crumble, an expression of complete surprise on his face.

Then Linda Raines called my name and I was gone.

THREE DAYS LATER

The second day, the doc let me have roast beef and mashed potatoes for dinner. My mother visited twice and told me that my father was a bit stronger than when I'd last seen him. Molly and Doran stopped by to tell me that they were off to New York to meet his editor and to find the nastiest lawyer available for his false-arrest suit against Cliffie. Jamie brought me the new issue of *Ellery Queen* and informed me that Turk wouldn't be suing me after all, because his lawyer wouldn't do anything until Turk paid off his bill. And since Turk was broke and Jamie wouldn't loan him any money, the suit was off.

Judge Whitney appeared all imperious and immediately began telling the nurses on the floor how to rearrange my room and complained that they weren't stopping in to check on me often enough. And Wendy brought me the newspaper that told of Reverend Cartwright's second failed attempt to destroy Beatles records.

LOCAL PASTOR NEARLY DROWNS; SAVED BY PROTESTOR

Yes, it seemed that Cartwright's attempt to start tossing albums and 45s off Indian Creek Hill turned disastrous when a strong wind came up and blew him right off the cliff and into the water sixty feet below. The only person thinking quickly and clearly enough to help him turned out to be one of the high-school boys who'd shown up to taunt him. The fifteen-year-old dove off the cliff, located the drowning pastor in the choppy water, and then swam him to the narrow shoreline, where he administered CPR. All that would be left for Cartwright now would be to order a nuclear attack on his ever-increasing mountain of Beatles material.

The third night, Wendy snuck in a sausage pizza and two cans of beer inside a shopping bag. It was fun hiding it all from the nurses. Wendy was really good at playing innocent, even though the two nurses who came by sniffed the air and looked at her suspiciously. Around eight thirty when one of the nurses popped back in to tell her that visiting hours were over, Wendy said that since we were getting married this coming weekend, she would appreciate it if she could stay in my room all night.

The nurse, an older sentimental soul, gave one of those smiles contestants on quiz shows do when they've just won a new Chevrolet. "That's very nice, miss. I'll tell the people at the desk so they'll let the night nurses know."

When she left I said, "That's a pretty expensive pizza. Marriage."

"Don't worry. I don't want to get married any more than you do, Sam. But I like having a boyfriend."

"So you wouldn't marry me even if I asked you?"

"Oh, God, you're not one of those, are you?"

" 'One of those'?"

"You know. You don't want to marry me until I say that I don't want to marry you, and then you want to marry me just so you can prove that I really wanted to marry you in the first place."

"Gee, I don't know what the hell you're talking about but, it sounds kinda fun."

"You know damned well what I'm talking about."

The nurse was back with half a dozen roses in a white glass vase. She placed it without ceremony on my rolling table. She plucked the tiny white card from it and handed it to me.

I scanned the words. I laughed so hard it hurt.

"Who's it from?" Wendy asked.

"Molly. She must've snuck off to send the flowers and write the card."

"What's it say?"

" 'Maybe I made a mistake. Last night he told me he knows John Lennon.' "

"That poor girl. He's probably an axe murderer."

Every few minutes I had to adjust my position in the bed. The pain from the wound wasn't as bad as it had been the first two days, but it helped to keep shifting the shoulder slightly.

She leaned forward in her chair and touched my hip. "Don't you see, Sam? All those serious affairs you had and nothing came of them? You got hurt or they got hurt or you both got hurt. I think you went at them too hard. I just want us to have the kind of thing we would've had in high school if I hadn't thought you were kind of a dork."

"You really thought I was a dork?"

"Well, Sam, you knew I was a snob. I was a cheerleader, for God's sake." She stood up then and leaned over so she could see me better. "You're not over loving Jane, and I'm not over being Bryce's second choice. We have to face it, so we may as well face it together. But we've got to take it slow.

That's all I'm saying."

"Dear Abby's got nothing on you."

"I'll bet Dear Abby never snuck a sausage pizza into a hospital."

Then she kissed me and said, "Will you be mad if I change my mind about staying all night? I just realized that that chair will cripple me for life if I try to sleep in it."

"You mean you wouldn't wrench your back out of shape even for love?"

She poked me in the chest and grinned. "Not even for love, bozo."

On the fourth day, they started me walking up and down the hall three times before dinner. On my second trip, I decided to do something useful. I stopped in to see William Hughes. His room was seven down from mine.

According to Wendy, he'd been shot in the chest and the left side. Lying in his hospital bed, reading a paperback copy of *The Spy Who Came in from the Cold,* his open blue pajama shirt revealed white tape around his chest and an IV drip positioned on his left arm. The room was bright with the Indian summer afternoon. Two small monitors sat on a tall thin table next to his bed. They made tiny bleating noises every five seconds or so. The medicinal smell was sharp but clean.

Hughes showed no particular interest when he looked up and saw me crossing from the doorway to his bed. He closed his paperback, stretched his arm across to the rolling table where he took his meals and kept his personal items. He grabbed a Zippo and a pack of Pall Malls. "The doctor comes in and gives me the big speech every time he sees the smokes." He had a grin that made you feel better about the world. He lighted his cigarette and clanked shut the top of his Zippo. In the sunlight I could see how much of his gray hair was turning white. I could also see that his burnished skin was more wrinkled than I'd realized. He was getting old.

"How're you feeling?"

"Now, how do you think I'd be feeling, McCain?"

"Stupid question, huh?"

"Very stupid."

"You planning to stay on with Linda?"

"I'm not sure that's any of your business. But she plans to sell the house and move on."

I nodded. I hesitated before I said it. It wasn't the kind of thing I wanted to think, let alone put into words. "Were you protecting him?"

The smoke he exhaled did a lovely blue dance in the sunbeams. Then he looked at me and said, "Why don't we cut the bullshit, McCain? You've got something to say to me, so why don't you say it."

"Maybe I just stopped in to see how you're doing."

"Oh, I'm sure that's true. I keep asking the nurses about how you're doing. We have something in common now, something we'll remember the rest of our lives. When Adair shot us. But that still leaves something unsaid, doesn't it?"

"We can always have this talk when you're feeling better."

"Just get to it, McCain. Right now."

I sighed. "If you knew Lou set up that fire, it was your legal duty to tell the law. You protected him because he saved your life. You committed a crime."

The head sank slowly back to the propped-up pillows. "The outfit I was with in Korea, bunch of racists. Used to taunt me all the time. I figured the gooks would probably treat me better than the assholes in my outfit did. So if one of *them* had had to save my life, I wouldn't be here today complaining about them. But Bennett — he was decent to me. I could tell I was sort of mysterious to him. Like somebody from outer space. But he was decent and if he caught somebody giving me a hard time, he shut him down right on the spot. The same with saving my life. He could've been killed right along with me. But he didn't care. He ran crisscross in front of all the gunfire and grabbed me and dragged me back to where I belonged. And he got me patched up enough so that I could hold out until they got a medic to take care of me. Bennett was some kind of half-assed medic himself. Did a damned good job on me. Damned good job."

He lolled his head to the right so he could see the table. He stabbed out his cigarette in a round tin ashtray. He left his head lolled like that, just staring at me. Something had changed in his demeanor. He wasn't as severe and formal as usual. And when he spoke, the language was a lot looser and friendlier.

"There I was with all these peckers picking on me because I was colored and I was half bleeding to death when Bennett went all heroic and rescued my ass and —" He smiled. "And I still didn't answer your question, did I?"

"No, no you didn't."

A deep sigh. He touched brown fingers to

the white tape. His face reflected pain. "Lou was shady. Took me a long time to figure that out. He ran on two tracks. There were the businesses everybody knew about, and then there were the businesses almost nobody knew about. He used a lot of different corporate names, so it was hard to trace any of it back to him. I put up with it. As far as I knew, nobody was being hurt. It was just — shady. Even when Roy Davenport got involved. Davenport was a mean son of a bitch, but I never knew about him actually hurting people. He did, of course. Maybe I forced myself not to realize that — you know, so I wouldn't turn against Bennett. But I happened to be around, the night that Raines and Davenport forced Bennett to write the letter admitting that he'd paid them to set the fire. They wanted it as insurance. They were afraid that Bennett had enough clout to set them up and turn them in. Later on, they started blackmailing him with it. That was when I couldn't handle it any more."

"You were friends with Karen."

"I was half-assed in love with her. Just like most men were."

"So what did you do?"

"I knew Davenport had the letter. I had to figure out where he kept it, and then I had to figure out how to get it. He'd just fired this secretary he'd been dallying with, and she was real, real pissed. I offered her five hundred dollars for the combination to his safe. I got the letter with no problem."

"What happened to it?"

"I put it in my safe deposit box in the bank. I'll turn it over to the law as soon as I leave here." His face was grim. "I didn't figure on anybody getting killed. That came out of nowhere."

"Maybe I should stop back."

The voice came from behind me. When I turned, I saw Mike Parnell in his wheelchair sitting outside the door.

"Hey, Mike, c'mon in." Hughes waved him in. Then to me, "Mike and me play shuffleboard over at Henry's Tap all the time. He's been up here every day visiting me."

Mike rolled in, right up to the bed. His new white T-shirt bore a vivid image of the American flag and beneath it, the slogan "The Blood of Heroes."

"You like hanging out with Commies, do you, William?"

"Oh, now, c'mon, Mike. You know what I told you. There's some people who just don't understand why we need to be over there. That doesn't make them bad people, that just makes them full of shit." I got the grin when he finished talking.

"Well, if there's one thing McCain is, it's full of shit. Always has been."

"So you two know each other?"

"Old friends," I said.

"*Used* to be old friends, you mean."

I guess it was the sudden tension. Or maybe it was just because I'd been standing for so long. The legs started to tremble and the head started to spin a little.

"I'm sorry, Mike. I feel like hell about it. I just think it's a mistake being over there."

Then I fell against the rolling table on the side of Hughes' bed.

A strong hand grabbed my forearm. "You all right?" Hughes said, still holding onto me.

"Just a little weak. I'd better get back to my room."

"Maybe I should call a nurse."

"No. I'll be all right. But I'd better get going."

I looked over at Mike in his wheelchair. I put out my hand. He wouldn't shake.

About halfway back to my room, I wished I'd asked Hughes to call for a nurse. I was sodden and chilled with sweat. The legs were weaker than ever.

By the time I reached my room, I was

staggering. I was so concerned with not falling over that I didn't realize Wendy had not only appeared but helped me to my bed.

"Real smart, Sam. What'd you do, run up and down the hall?"

But I was too fatigued to say anything. I drifted into a half sleep, aware that Wendy had been joined by a nurse. There was something about a sponge bath and something about sheets being changed and something about another IV drip. Then there was something about sleep.

Voices woke me. Man and woman. Both familiar.

When I rolled on my side and opened my eyes, I wasn't sure if what I saw was real. Wendy sitting in a chair next to my bed. Mike Parnell sitting in his wheelchair next to Wendy.

"I saw Mike in the hall. I wanted to tell him how much he hurt your feelings. Which was fine, because Mike wanted to tell me how much you hurt *his* feelings."

"You should be a cruise director."

"Very funny. Now I want you two morons to agree to disagree. I've invited Mike out to my place as soon as you get out of here and are able to have a little fun. We'll have some steaks and some liquor and we'll have a nice time. Mike's girlfriend will be joining us."

"I still can't believe you're going out with him," Mike said. "You were a cheerleader."

"I know. But times change. You have to make do with what's available."

"Yeah, but Sam McCain? You can't do better than that?"

"I know, it's terrible, isn't it? The worst thing of all is that I even started to like him. I like him quite a lot, actually."

Mike looked right at me and said, "I sure wouldn't admit it to anybody."

"I agree. Just please don't tell anybody what I said."

Shaking his head, Mike said, "Well, I need to leave. An hour and a half in a hospital is about all I can take." He reached over and patted Wendy's arm. "It's great seeing you again." He too had long lusted for the cheerleader. "Bye, Wendy."

"Bye, Mike. Remember my invitation."

He wheeled around in his chair and started rolling fast for the door.

"You're not going to say good-bye to me?" I said to his receding back.

He raised his right hand and without turning around gave me the bird. On his way toward the door, he said, "You're an asshole, McCain. You always were. I just never got around to telling you that when we were growing up."

Then he and his middle finger were gone.

"I'm sure we'll have a nice time when we all get together," Wendy said.

"Oh, yeah," I said, "as long as Mike doesn't bring a knife or a gun."

She laughed. "Well, at least he stopped in to see you." Then that cheerleader face of hers, so finely wrought despite the shadows of coming age we both bore, became mournful in the full flush of the sunlight. "I don't know what I'd ever do if I saw someone I love in a wheelchair because of some goddamn war. I've seen him around most of my life. Running and playing and horsing around. And now look at him. And for no good reason at all."

She started to cry, and I could see she was embarrassed. She managed a smile. "Listen to me, Sam, I sound just like you."

Then she leaned down and put her face into my neck and she slid her arms around me. Her skin was warm from her tears. She stayed like that for a while. Long enough for me to have the same pictures of Mike she had, of him running and jumping and horsing around.

Things he would never be able to do again.
And for no good reason at all.

We hope you have enjoyed this Large Print book. Other Thorndike, Wheeler, Kennebec, and Chivers Press Large Print books are available at your library or directly from the publishers.

For information about current and upcoming titles, please call or write, without obligation, to:

Publisher
Thorndike Press
295 Kennedy Memorial Drive
Waterville, ME 04901
Tel. (800) 223-1244

or visit our Web site at:

http://gale.cengage.com/thorndike

OR

Chivers Large Print
published by BBC Audiobooks Ltd
St James House, The Square
Lower Bristol Road
Bath BA2 3SB
England
Tel. +44(0) 800 136919
email: bbcaudiobooks@bbc.co.uk
www.bbcaudiobooks.co.uk

All our Large Print titles are designed for easy reading, and all our books are made to last.